THE GIRL
WHO MOTIVATED
MURDER MOST FOUL
By
J. Wayne Frye

The Author

Wayne Frye's *Aaron Adams*, *Girl* series books and *Lynton* adventures have been popular among Canadian mystery lovers since first appearing in 2005. He provides satirical political commentary to many Canadian newspapers, and his books on politics have created a great deal of controversy. He has written marketing/ advertising textbooks, been a successful U.S. university hockey coach, professor, university president and served as a marketing consultant to hockey teams and motion picture companies. He has been cited for his work with inner-city gang children in the Los Angeles area and been active in the anti-globalization movement. He became a Canadian citizen in 2003 and lives in Ladysmith, British Columbia and Cavite, Philippines.

Other Books by J. Wayne Frye

Hockey Mania and the Mystery of Nancy Running Elk
Something Evil in the Darkness at Hopkins House
How Hockey Saved a Jew From the Holocaust:
The Rudi Ball Story
The Catastrophic Calamities of a Village Idiot
Fighting for Justice in the Land of Hypocrisy
Guide to Alternative Education (13 Editions)
Cataclysmic Dreams in Black and White
The Girl who Stirred Up the Whirlwind
Introduction to Advertising
Fall From Apocalypse
Advertising Lab Manual
Promotions Workbook
Public Relations Workbook
Advertising Design
Armageddon Now
Worth
When Jesus Came to Jersey as the Son of Thunder
When Jesus Came to Canada to Lead an Indigenous Rebellion
Canadian Angels of Mercy – Nurses in Times of Peril
Points of Rebellion: Aboriginals Who Fought for Justice
Lynton Curls Her Hair
Lynton Buys a Cell-Phone and Hears the Voice of Doom
Chablis: Avenging Angel for the Forgotten in the City of Lost Hope

TABLE OF CONTENTS

TO: All those who have suffered the anguish of losing to another the one you love. It is a deep unimaginable hurt that tears at the soul.

JWF

This is a work of fiction. Any similarity to persons living or dead is coincidental.

Catalogue Number: 2014-2453566

ISBN: 978-1-928183-01-3

Fireside Books – Victoria, British Columbia

PROLOGUE
LIE DOWN WITH A MURDERER

He sat arrogantly on the commode as if he was a king and it was his throne. The door was open for his paramour to see and hear the most basic of human functions. His body reeked with odour. He had missing teeth as a result of drug addiction. The five days of growth made his scraggly beard look like the quills of a porcupine. His crop of thick black hair was unkempt and had flecks of lint from the bed all about it. He did not bother to thoroughly wipe his hair laden ass that also reeked with odour from two days of toilet use and no bath as the flakes of feces festered on the coarse hairs that traversed around his butt crack.

This was the man Jasmine Alexander Adams had left her husband for in a fit of rage over his temperament that she felt she could no longer endure. However, Brent McCord was more than just a hairy, unkempt lover. He was a man obsessed with the woman who had become infatuated with his calm, polite, seemingly submissive demeanour. However, beneath McCord's soft, sublime exterior beat the heart of a killer. As he rose from the commode, unceremoniously passing gas and burping, in his mind, he was contemplating murder. To thoroughly possess Jasmine, he had to eliminate a husband who still commanded a slight bit of love and compassion from a wife whose feelings had been stomped on in a vile fit of anger over a perceived indiscretion.

McCord was a man obsessed with not just winning Jasmine's love, but totally possessing her, placing her in a cocoon that would cut her off from those who might open her eyes to the machinations of control exhibited by a man with only one purpose in life – to make her his – body and soul. He must possess her, no matter what it required.

Jasmine had known murderers before, as she had been the woman written about in the best-selling book *The Girl Who Stirred Up the Whirlwind*. She had come up against the world's deadliest assassin and with the help of her champion, Aaron Adams; she had survived the ordeal unscathed. However, the *Whirlwind* could not hold a candle to Brent McCord when it came to sinister cunning and manipulative prognostications that bamboozled all who met him and assumed his mild demeanour and apparent shyness represented the real man. The real Brent McCord was a man with deep psychological problems that were manifested in the darkest recesses of a mind that was cold, calculating and determined to get what he wanted, regardless of the costs. This was a man capable of heinous acts when in pursuit of a woman who had simply captivated him.

On the other hand, Jasmine Alexander Adams was an unassuming woman who was easy prey for any man who offered her what she felt was missing from her life with Aaron Adams, the man who had saved her from the *Whirlwind*. She had been a loyal, devoted wife, until one day she simply decided that she could no longer tolerate what she saw as mood swings exhibited by a husband with deep psychological problems. Rather than standing by him as she always had, she abandoned him to the darkness that had been overwhelming him for years. Then again, who could blame her, as she had endured it for what she felt was far too long. Although Aaron had always been there when she needed him, and defended her like a noble knight in King Arthur's court, it simply was not enough to ease the pain she felt. Thus, she tossed aside her lovely home, her life of leisure and security to swoon in the arms of a man who had beguiled her with his reserved demeanour and manipulative charm.

She did not know that within this man's heart was a cruelty that came from the deepest recesses of hell. It was a determination born of fire and ash. It was an obsessive fascination with Jasmine that bordered on the psychotic, and it was now festering in his mind as he looked at the naked Jasmine standing by the electric skillet in her apartment, fixing breakfast for the man who was contemplating a most grievously foul act.

Jasmine turned toward Brent, her perky breasts shining in the morning light that filtered through the window. Her pert nipples erect with excitement as she thought of the coming fornicating, she smiled at this uncouth creature who was, unbeknownst to her, contemplating the murder of her husband, as he brazenly walked toward her, pulled her to his hairy, musky smelling body and made her melt with delight that he was about to plunge his manhood into her for the second time that morning. She was putty in the hands of a master at the manipulative arts. Little did she know that she was about to lie down with a murderer.

CHAPTER 1
ELIMINATE HIS ONLY RIVAL

In the beginning, there was sanity in small doses, but sanity nevertheless. However, as time passed, a mind deteriorated into a mere shell of its former self until a joyous and carefree life flowed into a river of mediocrity that spilled over a damn of lost hope. This was the beginning of murder most foul, as a plot was hatched in the mind of a deranged man to destroy Aaron Adams and claim his wife as a conquest.

Seeing Aaron as an old man who was weak in mind and body, Brent McCord immediately began to hatch a plot to get the beautiful Jasmine free of what he saw as an impediment to his conquest of the one woman who had captivated him like no other.

There is a difference between love and possession. When Brent McCord came into Jasmine and Aaron's lives, no one could have recognized the sinister intentions of a man who was about to be overcome with lust and infatuation over that which he never dreamed it was possible to possess. How these three met is a tale of woe, as Aaron unknowingly opened his door to the man who would not only steal his wife, but also be convinced that the only way to completely possess her was to eliminate Aaron.

Opening the door to your home can lead to good and ill. Aaron's fortune was foretold the day that he invited Brent into his home. Oddly enough, he had met Brent in McDonald's where they had casually talked about hockey. After awhile, Brent, who unbeknownst to Aaron, had already cast lustful eyes on his wife many times at hockey games they attended, had casually mentioned in their conversation how much he enjoyed piano music. Hearing that, Aaron, who was always proud of his wife's musical talent, invited him home to hear her play. This was the opening Brent had wanted for so long. Finally, he would meet the beautiful Jasmine Alexander Adams. Aaron was about to open his door to treachery.

When Aaron introduced Jasmine to Brent, she took a deep breath, smiled and tilted her head in the usual seductive way, and he knew that her deep brown eyes were opening the door to heaven. She seemed to satisfy every lustful desire Brent had ever had. She was a seductress that offered untold delights that were the stuff of legend in the community she and Aaron called home. She was young, though her wisdom spoke of knowledge only acquired with years. She was ripe, because though her experience was founded in thoughtful ferment, she was a creature of delight, pleasure, satisfaction, joy and bliss. Although reserved, she had a hedonistic nature that seemed to bubble to the surface with a slight hint of coyness that bespoke of a woman who was more tease than libertine.

She lit a flame in Brent's heart that kindled a raging fire of desire that immediately consumed him. It was all he could do to keep from dispatching Aaron with the vice-like grip of his muscular arms and sweeping her up to whisk her away into a liar where he could keep her captive only for him and his pleasure. There was a surge of vitalization in him accompanied by strength, energy, vigour and elasticity that made his heart pound with urgency. She had awakened a raging storm in an indolent man who before that moment had known only hopelessness and despair.

Looking at Aaron, he felt a surge of hatred and jealousy as he saw himself as one of the four horsemen of the Apocalypse. Yes, he saw himself as death with a scythe in hand to lay waste to all who stood between him and the woman he needed to possess. He would ride out of the fog-shrouded night to destroy that which he saw as an impediment to possessing that which had enthralled and captivated him. Death had come calling that night and neither Aaron nor Jasmine comprehended what was occurring.

Aaron had lived an often violent life as a result of his profession. Being a private investigator should have made him spot the evil before him, but for some reason, he was naïve about this man's intentions, and continued to ask Brent over to dinner and to go out with them to lacrosse and hockey games.

Aaron was opening the door to evil without knowing it. The man he let enter his home was uncouth, dirty of mind and body, unsophisticated, uncompassionate, malicious and cunning in seeking that which he wanted to possess at any cost.

Aaron feared no man, but he had never come up against a devil like this. This was not a man. This was an evil entity that was determined to destroy a marriage in order to possess that which made his blood race through his body like a river through a gorge. Nothing, absolutely nothing could stand in the way of his need to possess Jasmine.

Over the next three weeks, Jasmine, who had been denied the conjugal attention of Aaron for some time, was getting constant e-mails from Brent, who was teasingly telling her how much he admired her, and how he had fallen in love at first sight. Meanwhile, Aaron, who was beginning to sense that something was amiss, noticed that when Brent came over to visit one night he kept asking Jasmine to play the piano. As Brent sat beside her on the bench, Aaron noticed his hand kept moving closer to her exposed leg.

It was then that Aaron simply had enough. He walked over and said to Brent, "Get the hell out of our house and don't come back. We have made you welcome here and you have abused our hospitality with a crass display of inappropriate behaviour."

As Aaron escorted the now somewhat contrite Brent to his car in the parking arcade, he said, "You are persona non grata around here." Brent had no idea what that meant.

Brent was seething with anger, but held his temper and said nothing as he got into his car that was held together with duck tape and pulled out of the arcade. Aaron retuned to Jasmine who was still sitting at the piano. Staring daggers at Aaron, she said, "That was uncalled for. He was just being a typical man. Your mood swings are beginning to grate on me, and I am almost at the end of my rope. Brent is a sweet and gentle man who did not deserve that temperamental outburst from you."

Aaron, taken aback by his wife's defence of a man he found not only abhorrent but lacking in the simple rudiments of hygiene, replied, "How the hell can you defend that asshole. He was completely ignoring me while he treated you like a backstreet whore who was here for the taking. His deportment and manners are tasteless and crude. You are defending crassness."

"Since when do you have the right to decide who I can or cannot see? I find him charming in a crude sort of way. He is unsophisticated and unhygienic, but he treats me like a queen. You have been ignoring my needs for weeks as you cloister yourself in that room of yours in the throes of depression. I think it is time you looked in the mirror and realized that you are even more abhorrent than he is – at least in my eyes."

Aaron had never been talked to that way before by Jasmine. Her demure nature had always prevailed when they had arguments, but this was not the response he usually got from his dutifully loving wife. He tried to restrain himself but could not. A sudden verbal assault followed that would bring Jasmine to tears. However, she had been waiting for the right moment for years to rid herself of a man she was growing to despise. She had been with Aaron for 20 years, and the last three had seen him go steadily downhill psychologically as his mental state became more fragile. Rather than talk to him about it, she just endured it in silence, never bringing up his deep seated psychological problems or telling him that unless he agreed to get help that she was going to end what had been a generally happy union between two people who seemed uniquely suited for one another. Aaron hung his head and walked away as he endured the pain for the first time in his married life of questioning her faithfulness.

Distraught over the episode, Aaron simply lay on the sofa in his office staring at the ceiling, wondering what had led Jasmine to this point. Meanwhile, Jasmine went to her computer and immediately starting e-mailing not Brent, but another friend of theirs who had also voiced his intense interest in a romantic relationship with her. Suddenly, twenty years of fidelity seemed to be tossed aside as Jasmine went from the demure woman who worshipped Aaron to a sullen vixen now intent on seeking attention from as many men as possible. She was going to prove to herself that she did not need Aaron. She was about to embark on a journey into insidious infidelity.

What follows is as an accurate representation of the e-mails she started sending to any man who would pay attention to her. First was a friend of theirs named Adam Lowey. He was a mild-mannered, short, thin, meticulously dressed, and fastidiously hygienic extremely handsome Pakistani man who had befriended them after Aaron had given a speech to his criminology students at a local university. He had been enamoured with Jasmine and e-mailed her often without Aaron's knowledge. She had eschewed his advances in the past, but she now felt a strong urge to reach out to him. Jasmine was using Aaron's outburst of anger as an excuse to explore her options. She was approaching 50 and beginning to feel that the much older Aaron was not going to be able to give her the sexual excitement that she had been graving.

Jasmine: *How are you Adam?*

Adam: *How wonderful to hear from you.*

Jasmine: *I am lonely, and wish I had you here for company.*

Adam: *Where is Aaron?*

Jasmine: *He is in his damn office, sequestered from reality. His anger problems are causing me consternation. I need the arms of a strong man around me to give me a feeling of warmth and love. Know where I might find that?*

Adam: *You are asking me to be that man?*

Jasmine: *I love you Adam.*

Adam: *What?*

Jasmine: *I love you. I have loved you for a long time. Why don't I slip out of the house and meet you somewhere. Can you get away from your wife?*

Adam: *Jasmine, my wife would be suspicious if I left now, but you know what?*

Jasmine: *What?*

Adam: *I love you, too. I have since the first time I laid eyes on you.*

Jasmine: *I knew it Adam. I knew it all along.*

Adam: *My wife has me on a very short leash. She suspects me of having affairs with my students.*

Jasmine: *Well, can you blame her? You are a handsome, virile man.*

As the conversation continued, it became apparent to Jasmine that Adam was too cautious. Had Adam been more receptive to her manifestations of love, no doubt, he would have been the one Jasmine fell for, but his marital situation precluded him from being readily available. Now, Jasmine was desperate for the attention of a man, any man. Just then her instant message popped on. It was Brent. She bade Adam good-bye and immediately decided that Brent was not her first choice, but that he was certainly available.

Jasmine: *Hello there my love. I am sorry that you were run off, because I realize now that I have fallen in love with you.*

Brent: *And I with you my dear. I must see you and hold you in my arms.*

Jasmine: *I will arrange that as soon as I can. Would you like to take me to dinner one evening? Afterward we can go to your place.*

Brent: *You mean have a real date? Maybe even be sweethearts?*

Jasmine: *Yes, a man date; I want to date a real man. And you are certainly that. I can see it in your strong, muscular arms and your rugged unshaven face. You are a real man, not like Aaron who allows me to do as I please. I want a man who wants to envelope me in a cocoon of protection and keep me safe in his arms. Are you man enough to do that?*

Brent: *Baby, I am more man than you have ever had, don't let my calm demeanour fool you. I am gentle, but if anyone messes with my property, I will fight to the death to protect it. I will be the only man you will ever want from now on.*

Aaron would become the target of this man who was willing to do anything to possess Jasmine. By switching potential lovers, Jasmine had unintentionally set in motion a murder plot that would make Aaron a target for a sinister man and his accomplices who wanted to make the street run red with the blood of Aaron, whose only crime was loving a woman too much.

The intent of Brent to eliminate Aaron from the picture never occurred to Jasmine, as she naively believed that he was so passive and non-violent that he could never harm anyone. However, she would eventually find out that he could not only harm Aaron, but was capable of doing whatever it took to keep her under his control. That would not become apparent to her until she was already deep within his grasp and would be unable to break free of a man who had no mercy.

Thus, the infatuation and psychotic love of this seemingly mild mannered man would not only imprison Jasmine, but make Aaron a target for a most sinister and cruel plot by Brent to eliminate his only rival.

CHAPTER 2
ELIMINATE HIS ONLY RIVAL

Love is precarious. It can end in the flick of an eye. The deterioration of the relationship between Aaron and Jasmine had been slowly unravelling for three years before her ill-advised decision to run off with Brent. However, there was one seminal event that convinced Jasmine she must leave Aaron for her own sanity.

There was never any question in Jasmine's mind that Aaron loved her deeply. His devotion to her unequivocally made her feel like a queen on a throne where she was worshipped as a goddess. However, there were also times when Aaron would have mood swings and burst out with fits of anger. There was never any physical violence, but the tongue can often do more damage than fists.

One day, as Aaron drove her to a hair appointment, Jasmine mentioned that she wanted to spend some time away from him in order to gather her thoughts and try to analyze where she was headed with her life since she had just finished her Ph.D. Aaron, who had assisted her for three years in pursuing her dream, felt slighted and that his efforts on her behalf were unappreciated, because she wanted to be free of him for a few days. In his warped mind, he saw this as an act of betrayal.

Suddenly, he had a violent, vindictive outburst. "Goddamn, I have spent the last 20 years making your life all it could be. I have provided you with love, guidance and always lifted you up from the depths of despair. I was there by your side when all others deserted you. I stood by you when others looked on you with disdain. I forsook my friends, my career, all my personal needs to serve at the altar of your love. Who was there when you were ill and needed an operation? Who was the first person you gazed upon after that operation? Who bought you clothes? Who fed you? Who provided you with new cars? Who took you anywhere you wanted to go? Who reached out to you and embraced you to ease your fears and pain? Who was as much a father to you as a husband? Who has provided you with guaranteed security in your old age through frugality and wise investing? I have never done for myself, because my mission is to take care of you. Are you blind to all I have tried to do for you? Goddamn! Goddamn!" he cried as he pounded on the steering wheel, shouting violently.

Jasmine said not a word, but as Aaron looked at the hurtful scowl on her lips, his violent outburst slowly subsided, and he sensed this was a seminal event that would forever alter their relationship. He did not say it, but he knew. Yes, he knew that deep within she was fighting to keep her own sanity as he seemed to be losing his.

Thus, this was the day that Jasmine decided to abrogate her love, to throw away security, to toss 20 years of Aaron's affection and devotion into the dustbin of forgotten hope. It was not as tough as she thought it would be. However, it would eventually prove to be an ill-thought out sojourn into the arms of a man who would not only want to destroy Aaron, but to bring her under the iron-fisted grip of controlling passion that would eventually strangle and suffocate the free spirit that made her unique among women. This would be a nightmare for Aaron, but it would also lead Jasmine into the arms of a man who could give her no hope, no direction and place her into a pit of despair that she simply could not see looming on the horizon, because she would be blinded by love, without realizing that which she perceived as love was possessive obsession by Brent. Jasmine would free herself of Aaron's mood swings, but she would find herself in the arms of another man who, though not suffering from mood swings, was actually more depressed than Aaron ever was, and this depression would manifest itself with a violent fury that would rival war in its ferocity. This fury would be aimed at destroying Aaron, eliminating him as a rival for Jasmine's affection, bringing him to the altar of evil to be gutted and destroyed. The evil in what appear to be good men's hearts can be well hidden from those too naïve to look beneath the surface. Ah, but it was there within Brent.

The Girl Who Motivated Murder Most Foul

That day, as Aaron dropped Jasmine off at the hairdressers and watched her walk into the salon, he felt a deep sense of foreboding disaster on the horizon. He thought to himself in rhyme:

> *Thinking of you and all that was, and all*
> *That might have been and never will be,*
> *I feel your honoured excellence, and see*
> *Myself unworthy of the happier call.*
> *For woe is me who is so apt to fall,*
> *So apt to shrink afraid, so apt to flee,*
> *Apt to lie down and die. Ah, woe is me!*
> *Your faithlessness turns me to the wall.*
> *I am hopelessly lost in the quiet,*
> *Tossing and turning each night.*
> *Sick each morning, wrestling with the break,*
> *It often seems more than I can take.*
> *I still bask in your grace as best I can,*
> *Ready to fight and die for your sake.*
> *Ah, if I could only rekindle the flame,*
> *To get your love for me to proclaim.*

Picking her up at the hair salon, all seemed to be forgotten, but beneath the surface, Jasmine was contemplating her next move. She was secretly planning an exit from Aaron's life, but she would play a game of subterfuge until she was ready. It would happen on her terms. This was a woman who was now erecting an emotional barrier between her and Aaron. That barrier would be a wall of discontent.

The next few days were shared in relative joy, but Jasmine was aching to free herself from what she felt was an untenable situation. Meantime, Aaron who was always looking out for her welfare, decided that it was his duty to procure her a job, because she had voiced a deep desire to go to work after finishing her Ph.D. Although she had not worked in the 20 years they had been together, Aaron felt that it was incumbent upon him to find her a position in which she could not only feel useful, but prosper and grow as a person. A Ph.D. in social work does not guarantee anyone employment, but Aaron sat out to find that which would make Jasmine feel useful and productive. After all, he had tutored and guided her through her Ph.D. programme, and helped her conduct the research that led to her dissertation being praised as a remarkable work of scholarship that was even published by a New York City publisher that saw tremendous commercial possibilities in it. She had graduated at the top of her class through sheer will power on her part.

Aaron began contacting a variety of places that were advertising for a skilled social worker. He knew that he might have to sacrifice his career for hers, but at almost 70 years of age, he felt that perhaps it was time to retire anyway. E-mailing places all over New York, the responses were overwhelming when employers realized the abilities of this remarkable woman. Although it was Aaron who procured the interviews though his tenacity, it was Jasmine's demeanour and quiet confidence that made each organization eager to procure her services, because she was willing to work places where others simply were not interested in going. Younger people preferred the city, but she was prepared to give that life up to work in rural areas where skilled social workers were much harder to find. Ironically, through it all, as job offer after job offer come in, Aaron was planning the rest of their life together in an isolated area where they would live in eternal bliss. He naively believed that he was about to enter his most sanguine period with Jasmine in an area outside the city, free of that disgusting man, Brent, who seemed to always be on her mind as evidenced by the frequency with which she would bring him up. Yes, maybe Aaron could once again kindle the flame of love that seemed to still be there, but was not the bright light that once shown in the darkness of his diseased mind.

How cloistered in unreality is the mind that loves intensely, that cannot see the deterioration of compassion and love. As Jasmine voiced her love and affection for Aaron, he could not comprehend her ever leaving him. Yet, she was continually corresponding with a variety of men for whom she pronounced affection. Each night as she lay in bed with Aaron, gently wrapping her arms around him, she was plotting her escape from that which she now saw as a pit of despair. This wilful deceit she felt necessary to carry out her escape.

Although she was eager to be free of Aaron, she callously plotted to hide her desire to flee from him as she cloaked herself in a mask of pretended affection for a man she still had feelings for, but loathed at the same time. Hers was a lonely battle of deception as she prepared to explore all avenues of escape.

Accepting a job in upstate New York in a rural area filled with farms, Jasmine was excited about the possibilities that lay before her. However, she also felt an intense tingling between her legs as she thought of what it would be like to be free of Aaron, free to explore her sexuality which had often been neglected by Aaron, who with age and taking medication that restricted his libido, had been unable to supply that which Jasmine craved. In fact, she had begun to doubt her own sexuality? Could men still find her appealing? Could she still fornicate with wild abandon as she once did? Yes, she needed affirmation as a woman, and sex would give her that.

Skilfully manipulating Aaron to take her to the new job, but urging him to return to their home and prepare it for sale while closing up his business in the city, she was preparing for trysts with men to affirm her womanhood.

Time flies, hope flags, life plies a wearied wing.
Youth and beauty gone, what doth remain?
Silence of love that seems it cannot sing again.

Unaware of the impending doom before him, Aaron foolishly believed that all was well, and that his life with Jasmine was about to enter a new phase in a new place. However, in the tiny rural town of Finger Lake, while a lonely Aaron was back in the city, Jasmine was furiously on her computer in search of those "man dates" that she wanted so badly in order to see if she was still appealing.

She reflected on the aging Aaron, and mused on long ago when he had refused to marry her for the first three years they were together, because of the age difference. And he had been right, because he said the time would come when the age difference would matter, though it might not at that particular time. Now it did. Although Jasmine felt bad, leaving an aging man who would probably never again know love, she was exhilarated by the attention she was receiving, and felt justified because of Aaron's mood swings. The vows she took "for better or worse" seemed but a distant memory.

The very first night she was alone in Finger Lake she arranged on-line for a date with a 55 year old man who bragged about his successful real estate empire. Not particularly impressed with him, she still thought it wise to get back in the dating game as soon as possible. That night, as Aaron sat at home pining for his beloved wife, she came to her apartment from work and spent three hours preparing for her first real date in 20 years. She was as giddy as a teenager as she could feel moisture forming between her legs.

Milton was a tall, robust, fairly handsome 55 year old man who, in his $2000 suit, actually cut a rather dashing figure. Although not overwhelmed with interest, Jasmine did find him mildly intriguing as they went to a nearby upscale restaurant for dinner.

In a small town, tongues can often wag like the tail of an excited dog. In the small community where Jasmine was, the one nice restaurant was a place where the gossips of the community were known to congregate. That night, unaccustomed to seeing a woman of Jasmine's beauty, poise, bearing and charm, the eyes of all present, including the staff, gazed with disbelief at the magnificence of the woman who strolled in with the immaculately attired gentleman from a nearby city. The man, with Jasmine on his arm, strutted through the restaurant like a peacock with crystal plumage to where he and Jasmine took a seat in a far back booth. The man actually felt ego gratifying euphoria as all eyes seemed to be turned toward them. The people were impressed with his taste in women, and he was already captivated by Jasmine. In his mind, he thought to himself, "I shall possess this woman and make her mine. By doing so, I shall be the envy of all."

Unfortunately, this man was unaware that Jasmine was simply on a sexual adventure, seeking avenues of delight and affirmation of her womanhood that she had not experienced in years. Also, in the back of her mind was Brent. She had experienced a special delight with this unkempt, provincial, pedestrian, uncouth, unsophisticated cretin who seemed to, for some unknown reason, excite her and make her feel like a bitch in heat. As she sat there trying to feign interest in the pompous, arrogant real estate tycoon, she kept thinking about Brent. He was uneducated, unhygienic and couldn't rub two nickels together, as he had spent his life in a drug stupor spending every dime he made foolishly thinking that happiness had a price tag. For that reason, he lived day-to-day with no thought of what tomorrow might bring. His idea of security was having enough gas in his car to get to the liquor store on Friday nights to buy the weekend euphoria in a bottle that had replaced his drugs that had been his escape from the reality of a life spent on the edge of an abyss that always seemed to be pulling him in. Yet, Jasmine found herself strangely attracted to this creature of instant gratification.

That night, as she sit listening to the real estate magnate brag about his accomplishments, she pleaded for him to take her home, but his arrogance and pleasure in being with her, made him linger until the place closed at 11:00 o'clock. Realizing she had to be up for work in six hours, Jasmine thought that she would simply invite him in to her apartment, dazzle him with her incredible oral talents and send him on his way. Unfortunately, she always underestimated her mesmerizing power over men, who all seemed to instantly fall in love with her. After she finished what she thought would be the chore that would lead to his exit, he was even more enamoured. He simply refused to leave, crawling in bed with her and insisting he spend the night. Too tired to argue, Jasmine agreed and fortunately, because of his age, he was so exhausted from Jasmine's dazzling performance that he instantly fell asleep. However, the next morning, he was encouraging her to let him get her a nicer place, even hinting that he would buy her a home. Like so many bombastic braggarts, the truth was, although he made lots of money, when it came right down to it, he offered no more security than Brent did, because he lived an excessively lavish lifestyle that necessitated often borrowing money just as Brent did, to get through to his next payday, and for him, depending on the "big deal" that was just around the corner probably put him into an even more precarious position than Brent.

Dates with three other men that week actually made Jasmine weary of the whole routine, so weary that she was beginning to ask herself if she wouldn't be better off with Aaron, who was not arrogant and self-absorbed, but saw through the shallowness of those who thought their wealth and power made them more desirable. However, Jasmine's consideration of her folly would be interrupted by a man who had even more insidious intentions than the four men she had dated that week. The real estate tycoon was a master marketer who wowed people with his gift of gab, unlike Brent who could not put two intelligent sentences together. However, Brent was better at using his tendency to be morose to get what he wanted from Jasmine. A contractor she dated was a master at complimenting her on her knowledge of architecture. However Brent used his lack of knowledge as an inducement to make her think he admired her intelligence.

The banker she dated tried to dazzle her with financial terms that he thought made him seem more intelligent. On the other hand, Brent used his ignorance of finances to make Jasmine feel sorry for his plight in life.

Then, there was the Muslim professor she dated who was actually pretty nice, but he could never stop bringing Allah into the conversation, even while they were having sex. He went so far as to justify infidelity by proclaiming that God approved of men having the freedom to engage in sexual peccadilloes. Yet, his gentlemanliness and gracious manners made Jasmine swoon with utter delight every time she was around him.

Brent, on the other hand, used his lack of education to ingratiate himself to a woman who was obviously his superior in wit, sophistication and intellect. So, of all the men she could have fallen for, she picked the one who would be most destructive to her psyche and lead her, through his manipulative crying every time she seemed to be moving away from him, to keep her in his grasp.

Brent was a man who possessed no real social graces, but he was a man who knew how to ingratiate himself to others through a demure manner that was all act and no substance. He had simply mastered the art of making people think he was something much more than he really was. Unsophisticated, inarticulate, unshaven, unkempt, unhygienic and crude in his mannerisms he still was a master of the manipulative arts. This was a man who appeared to be to be humble, quiet and unassuming. However, he was more than what just appeared to the naked eye. This was a stridently homophobic, impetuous manic-depressive man with insidious, diabolical, violent intentions aimed at procuring that which he wanted to possess at all costs, and a naïve Jasmine was going to fall into his web of deceit and make Aaron a target for murder.

CHAPTER 3
HATED HER ENOUGH
TO COMMIT MURDER

Did he endeavour to possess,
An elegance of mind that did not exist
To lure his ornament, and know how to please
With uncouth grace and insidious ease?
Beware the wolf in sheep's clothing
Because in his trickery, she, he is molding
To fall into his lover's trap so bold
That falsely sparkles like gold.
His heart appears true, but it is made of stone.
So jealous of her, he will not leave her alone.
Making sure she is under his thumb,
He makes her answer to his anthem.
She is confused about love and is now trapped,
Because in his deceitful web she is wrapped.
Still her champion of old will not bend in the wind,
No matter how much he is chagrined.
Hope springs eternal in his emptiness,
That she will escape from the darkness.

After a week of going on her infamous man-
dates, Jasmine decided to answer some of Brent's
mountain of e-mails begging her to let him visit
her in Finger Lakes, now that she was free of
Aaron, who was stuck in the city closing up his
business. She could not figure out what the
attraction to this uncouth, unmannered, crude,
unhygienic man was. Yet, she found herself

wanting to know what it would be like to have sex with such a man. She dreamed of unbridled, hedonistic, wild fornicating with a rugged individual who had no manners, no breeding and often had trouble finding the shower. Damn, she felt the moisture building between her legs and even her nipples perked up. She agreed to lie to Aaron to make sure that he did not come out to see her that weekend, so that she could devote all her time to wild fornicating. There was no guilt in her mind, as she turned her back on the man who had been her protector, her confidant, her knight in shining armour. She was now intent on tossing Aaron aside, discarding an old man who had simply out lived his usefulness in her world, where her emotionless, aloof and detached clinical approach to all things had simply hardened her heart toward the one man who had always been her champion. Now, she longed for the rugged man who had lusted after her for so long.

That Friday night Brent showed up at Jasmine's apartment in his taped up car, eager to take her out to dinner and lavish her with affection. Unshaven, belly hanging out over his belt because he had on a dirty T-shirt that would not completely cover it, he smiled with glee when Jasmine met him at the door, reached up and kissed him lightly on the lips. It was all he could do to restrain himself from sweeping her into his arms and whisking her into the bedroom. Yet, he realized that using a subtle, more restrained approach would make her think he was a gentleman of quality and distinction. He must first get her trust and convince her that he was special. That way, he could ultimately exercise the control that would make her his and trap her in his web of deceit.

Although most people would, on first glance, pass this unkempt, ill-at-ease man off as just a dumb working stiff who had never accumulated anything because of his drug addiction, lack of education and no acumen for how to handle money, the truth was much deeper. Despite being a man who was always teetering on the edge of a financial cliff, he was much smarter than he looked when it came to manipulating women with his demure "ah shucks" attitude that usually endeared women to him.

Most people looked at the two of them and could not believe that a woman as culturally refined, as educated, as beautiful as Jasmine would be romantically involved with a man who had no social graces, looked dirty, always had lint in his uncombed mop-like hair and had teeth that were missing or browned from drug use. Jasmine, herself, kept wondering what she saw in this uncouth creature who belched and passed gas in her presence with no embarrassment whatsoever. What was his hold on her? That weekend, she would discover that one of the biggest holds was the magnificent member between his legs that brought her hour after hour of intense carnal pleasure like she had rarely experienced in her life. And damn, did he know how to use that love tool.

They spent most of the weekend frolicking in a fornicating frenzy in bed, but as each day progressed, this master manipulator kept weaving his spell to capture Jasmine in his web of deceit, making sure that she was well-aware of the kind, caring, reserved demeanour that he always displayed coyly in her presence. Then, on a trip to the mall, the first of many machinations of control began to occur.

So enamoured with his quiet, somewhat shy demeanour, Jasmine did not even realize what was happening when he told her that he wanted to get her a cell-phone so she would always know that she could get in touch with him if she needed him. "How thoughtful" said Jasmine. Unfortunately, she was naïve about his real intentions. The real purpose of the phone was to make it possible for him to keep tabs on a woman whom he feared might be seeing other men. His insistence that she be available for him to call every morning, every day at noon, every afternoon at 4 and every night at 9:30 was his way of keeping her from being able to ever be free of his control. This was the beginning of the strangle-hold that he would exercise to make certain she never had a chance to be free of him.

It was also at this time that Jasmine began to have some minor doubts herself about a man who constantly voiced his distaste for homosexuals. This particularly grated on Jasmine's sensibilities, because she was open-minded and accepting of varied lifestyles, and she, herself, had once been in love with her beloved Rose in Stockholm before she was killed by the infamous assassin, the *Whirlwind*.

Brent spent lavishly on her; seemingly buying her everything that he thought would endear her to him. Once, when Jasmine said her back hurt, he said, "Then I'll get you a new mattress, that one is useless." Despite her pleas to not do it, while she was at work the next day, he had a $3000 mattress delivered. Jasmine was overwhelmed with the way he spent money.

Little did Jasmine know that the reason he rode around in a car held together by duct tape was due to an inability to manage money. Everything he was buying was bought on a credit that would necessitate years to pay off. This was a man who simply believed in instant gratification with no concern for tomorrow. Above all, he believed Jasmine was ``Buy-Sexual`` - all you had to do was buy her something and the sex was yours. He was too stupid to see that she never based her feelings on the amount money a person had, because if she had, Brent would have never gotten through the front door. Still, he felt that he had to compete with the more successful Aaron, so he foolishly squandered thousands of dollars in pursuit of what was becoming an obsession. This was not just any woman. This was the woman he would make his wife, because that piece of paper signified ownership in his warped mind.

Now, it is important to point out that Brent, although professing his willingness to use unbridled violence against anyone who would do Jasmine harm or against any man who might try to steal that which he now thoroughly considered his property, he had never indicated any other tendencies toward violence. However, one incident would make a small seed of doubt about Brent's violent streak begin to germinate and grow in Jasmine's mind. It would involve Jasmine's best friend, who decided to visit her one weekend in Finger Lakes.

Denise had known Jasmine for almost 10 years and Jasmine knew a dark secret that no one else was privy to, because of Denise's intense fear of discovery. Yes, Denise lived in mortal fear that her new boyfriend would discover a secret that she had kept hidden for many years. Denise was a post-op transsexual.

Jasmine had always reassured her that the secret was safe with her, and Denise knew that Jasmine's integrity precluded anyone from ever finding out from her. Yet, Denise loved a man who was homophobic, provincial and had no tolerance for alternative lifestyles. She came to Jasmine for guidance, as Jasmine was also dealing with a boyfriend who exhibited the same qualities, but fortunately Jasmine had no such secret to mar her psyche. So, she was beginning to find out what it was like to be with a man who was closed minded and unaccepting of alternative lifestyles. The two women calmly discussed if Denise should reveal the dark secret that she had kept hidden from everybody but her immediate family. Should she stop her deception and reveal the truth?

Jasmine very calmly said, "Denise, if you love him, you cannot hide this any longer as it is a deceitful barrier that will forever condemn you to despair over what he would do if he ever found out, and someday, somehow he will find out. It may be tomorrow. It may be next week, next month or 20 years from now, but someday something will happen – a slip of the tongue, a visit to the doctor's office, an accident or any number of things. If he genuinely loves you, it should make no difference. Your fear of him reacting harshly is indicative that you are vacillating on whether there is really any depth of love there from him, but also from you. How could you love a man who could not accept you? There is no real love if you live in fear? You should never fear the one whom you love."

The two of them continued to talk for hours, until the sun came up over the horizon, heralding another day – a day that would lead to the death of someone near and dear to Jasmine, a death that was only the beginning of a violent interlude that would shake the very foundations of several people's lives, causing a cascade of events that rivaled war in its intensity.

Since it was the weekend, Jasmine's new found love, Brent, as he did every weekend, insisted on coming to spend Friday and Saturday nights with her in the small cottage she was renting. How could she say no? He called her every morning, every day at 4 when he got off work, and, of course, every night at 9:30 to be sure she was not with any other men. Between those times he was constantly e-mailing or texting.

How could she be with another man? He was constantly checking up on her. Still, Jasmine found his infatuation endearing, but over time she would see the controlling mannerisms as a threat to her independence as a woman. He was so in love with her, and she was now falling in love with him, or was she falling for the large penetrating love muscle that gave her the sexual ecstasy she graved? She began, subconsciously, to analyze the difference between lust and love. Unfortunately, she would not truly understand the difference in time to prevent some dramatic events that would lead to a raging fire of passion that would nearly destroy everything in its path.

Denise had always been leery of meeting people for fear that, as her compatriots said; she would be "clocked." When Jasmine introduced her to Brent, she felt great trepidation about a man who seemed quiet, respectful, reserved and malleable on the outside, but there was something beneath that calm exterior that bothered her. She realized Jasmine was fascinated with him and did not want to mention the feelings to her. Yet, she had a sense of impending doom. Was it her doom, Jasmine's or both?

Denise had always admired Aaron, because he treated her like a lady, and never broached the subject of her being a transsexual, despite the fact that he was privy to the truth. Aaron was a man who simply refused to be socially judgmental in any way. He believed that dignity should be extended to all. He knew that what was between a person's legs did not define gender. This attitude, however, was a trait Brent had trouble with, because he saw anyone who deviated from the norm as repugnant. Still, although stubbornly bound to convention, he often found himself fantasizing about a sexual liaison with a man. The limited latitude he afforded himself simply locked him into a cell of ignorance in a jail of the mind that imprisons so much of humanity.

After being introduced to Denise, Brent immediately felt some trepidation about her. She did not seem to be the usual woman in appearance and mannerisms. She had thick, broad shoulders, a manly voice, large hands and feet. At 6:2, she was much taller than Brent. Then there was her prominent Adam's apple. The unsophisticated, uneducated, provincial Brent knew that Jasmine was open-minded and accepting. If he was going to convince her of his sincerity, he would have to make sure that he did not seem to pass judgment on Denise, but deep within, he had already decided that she was a freak.

That night, Brent was preparing for the fornicating ritual that was the thread that bound the cloth of his love for Jasmine. As always, Jasmine prepared her body meticulously for lovemaking. As she stepped out of the shower, she lit up the room with her radiance.

How does on adequately describe a Venus. Jasmine, her long, lustrous hair cascading down over her front shoulders enough to hide the perky nipples on her huge globular breasts stood defiantly naked before Brent who scanned her tantalizingly provocative body, taking in every gorgeous curve. Although shapely, her belly protruded a bit, but on her it was an enhancement not a detriment. The huge navel made Brent contemplate dumping a load of his joy juice into it to see if it might actually overflow and glow on her deep brown skin. As he gazed slightly lower, there it began – the unbridled road to paradise. A thin, black line of coal-black hair started at the very bottom of her navel and stretched downward toward a huge mound of thick black coarse pubic hair that stretched all the way to her thick, gorgeously seductive thick thighs. Ah, but that hair around her mound of desire made Brent want to bury his face in it so he could sniff it, kiss it and worship it. It beckoned like a siren of the sea luring sailors to their doom, but this was not an object of fear. The only fear was that one might be deprived the privilege to taste its nectar. Yes, the nectar of Jasmine was calling – calling all men who desired a real, genuine woman with no inhibitions.

After hours of frantic lovemaking, Brent lay there and could not resist saying, "that friend of yours is sort of freaky. She seems more like a man than a woman. She even has an Adam's apple. Is she really a woman?"

"Of course she is a woman. She has always been a woman."

Brent, now completely puzzled, replied, "Yeah, like I am a woman. She is a transvestite. I know she is."

Jasmine, unaccustomed to people who were judgmental, said, "She has always been a woman in her mind. A while ago she became a woman in body as well. Don't be closed-minded. You must try to reach out with compassion to people. She suffers from a disease. It is called gender dysphoria. It afflicts many people, and thanks to modern science, it can now be corrected.

Despite his ignorance, Brent wanted to understand, because he felt it would endear him to Jasmine. His sole purpose was to mesmerize her with his kindness and to make her understand his intense love for her. However, he was more obsessed than in love. He was unable to discern the difference, and that would eventually prove deadly.

It was Saturday morning around 8:00 AM when Brent crawled out of bed as Jasmine lay sleeping, put on his pants, smiled down at his massive organ of delight and nonchalantly sauntered down the hallway and greeted Denise as she was stepping through the doorway to her bedroom.

Brent said, "Good morning" as he passed her, let out a belch and passed gas. Denise, shocked at the man's uncouth manners, could hardly manage a "hi" in return due to the shock of observing such an ill-mannered person. She watched him arrogantly walk into the bathroom, leave the door ajar, unzip his pants and sit down on the toilet, like it was his kingly throne, to noisily relieve his bowels.

How, thought the mannerly, prim and proper Denise, could Jasmine find such an unmannerly, despicable man appealing? Denise found him disgusting.

It was then that Denise made a decision that would unravel the fragile mind of Brent. She loved Jasmine dearly, but loved Aaron also. She had assured Jasmine, due to their friendship, that she would not reveal her romantic interlude with Brent to Aaron. However, she found herself so repulsed by the man that she felt it a necessity to warn Aaron about what was going on. Someone had to rescue Jasmine from the grips of this despicable creature, and Aaron was a man who loved his wife so much that he would not harm her, but rather, reach out with compassion to talk some sense into her. After all, Jasmine had always relied on him to keep her from harm. Surely Jasmine could be shown that Brent was simply too unhygienic, uncouth and disgusting to warrant her romantic attention. Yes, she would see the folly of her fascination.

Denise quietly dialled Aaron's number, and as she did, Brent was standing in the hallway intent on listening to what was being said as he suspected that Denise was up to something. Aaron did not answer the phone. Denise left a message, and Brent heard her plea to Aaron, "This is Denise, get up here right away, Aaron. There is a situation that demands your attention."

Those words were Denise's death warrant. A seething rage flushed over Brent. He hated what Denise was, and now she had even gone so far as to warn Aaron that something was going on between him and Jasmine. He was going to kill the bitch, and when he finished with her, he would dispatch Aaron Adams as well. The first murder would be easy, the second a bit more complicated, but nothing could stand in the way of his ultimate goal. He would own Jasmine's mind, body and soul. In fact, with Aaron out of the picture permanently, he would insist on marriage and even wind up with half of Aaron's considerable assets. That marriage licence was important, because in Brent's warped mind, it signified ownership, and he would own this woman who was now all that mattered in his worthless life that had been spent in a drug stupor and in the relentless pursuit of pleasure through throwing money away like it grew on trees. Brent called this infatuation with Jasmine love, but it was not. It was the insidious evil of obsession.

As Denise hung up the phone, Brent burst into her room, and before she could let out a scream, he hit her across the face with a sledgehammer like motion from his massive fist. Denise collapsed to the floor unconscious. Brent bent over, took the pillow from the bed and held it over Denise's face, smiling, as he pressed so hard that he could feel her nose breaking under the pressure. He felt a great exhilaration as the life flowed out of her. He picked up the limp body, tossed it over his left shoulder and walked through the kitchen and out the back door. He hurriedly walked up the hillside that led to a bluff over the rock-littered lakeshore below. Knowing that the coroner's verdict would be an accident from falling off the cliff, he tossed her body onto the rocks below. Damn, he actually felt good!

He walked back into the house and went into Jasmine's bedroom where he just stood, staring at down at her naked body, as she was sleeping peacefully. Her dark brown silky smooth skin seemed to cry out for the touch of a virile man, and Brent was certainly that. His huge, throbbing member had penetrated every orifice Jasmine offered. He had even playfully shoved it into her ears, teasingly promising that she would be the sole recipient of his joy juice that spurted out from the uncut hose of euphoria that titillated Jasmine like no other man's member whom she had ever experienced.

Brent almost laughed out loud as he realized that he had conquered the unconquerable. That which he never dreamed of possessing was now completely, totally, unabashedly his. Well, almost his. One thing stood in the way – Aaron Adams, and he would take care of that problem in due time in a way that was already forming in his warped mind. He would have to leave Jasmine for a short while, as Aaron and the authorities would soon be there; then, after time, he would arrange to take care of Aaron. Yes, Denise was only his first victim.

As he said good-bye to Jasmine, she asked if he had seen Denise. Brent coyly replied, "I saw her go out the kitchen door and head up the pathway to the cliffs. She is just out for some fresh air I am sure."

Jasmine looked out the kitchen window up toward the cliff and a dark cloud passed over the sun, bathing the landscape in darkness. Jasmine felt emptiness, and she did not think about Brent then. Rather, when trouble seemed to be brewing, her thoughts turned to Aaron, her champion. With Brent by her side, she felt uneasiness. He simply wasn't Aaron. Nobody could help her when she was troubled like Aaron could. Was she having second thoughts about Brent and leaving Aaron? Aaron always offered her hope, and an escape from darkness.

There was never any question about Denise's death being an accident. At the funeral, Aaron reflected back on how he had first met Denise. Jasmine had introduced them, and Aaron could not help but snicker under his breathe at this person who was trying so hard to be a woman. However, the cockeyed wig, the atrocious five o'clock shadow, the husky voice, the muscular broad shoulders, the prominent Adam's apple and the manly swagger betrayed her.

Jasmine wanted to help her have the looks and demeanour of a woman, but she did not want to embarrass her. For that reason, she was very tenuous with suggestions. Aaron's treatment of Denise was one of the early indications to Jasmine he was a man with a deep sense of compassion and understanding. Regardless of how she looked, Aaron always treated her like a lady. He knew that it was the mind, not the body that defined gender. Aaron was a man who saw through the indifference and judgmental arrogance of those who thought themselves morally superior. To Aaron, this was the very height of hypocrisy.

Aaron simply believed that if you were harming no one, you should be left alone to be master of your fate and captain of your soul. For that reason, he had always treated Denise with respect. One evening, when he took Jasmine and Denise to a dance club, he observed Denise gyrating to the music, and obviously wanting to dance. However, because of her cockeyed wig and ridiculous looking makeup and apparel, no man dared even talk with her. It was obvious to Aaron that she longed for a man to recognize her as a woman and ask her to dance.

Aaron, sensitive to the fragile nature of a woman who was struggling for acceptance in a world where the religious paragons of virtue and pontificators of judgmental arrogance ruled supreme, walked over to Denise, smiled and said, "May I have the pleasure of this dance?"

From that moment on, Denise literally worshipped Aaron, because he was the first man to ever genuinely treat her like a woman. That love and concern for Aaron had gotten her killed by a man who had deep-rooted hatred for what he saw as an abomination.

Denise had felt it her duty to warn Aaron about what was happening to Jasmine, who had turned her back on Aaron and given her heart, mind, body and soul to a man with deep character flaws.

That night in the dance club, Jasmine, upon seeing Aaron's grand gesture, felt a surge of respect for a man who had just begun to capture her heart. She had seen the rough exterior of a man whose profession seemed to necessitate callousness, but she saw Aaron that night as a man capable of deep, abiding compassion. It had endeared him to her. However, that endearment would fade over the years and now, unbeknownst to Aaron, Jasmine was the paramour of another man. However, at the funeral, Jasmine sat in the second row of the church, leaning forlornly on Aaron's shoulder. In times of turmoil, no one but Aaron could console her. He was the rock upon which she could rest, safe in the knowledge that he would always be there to protect her. Taking a deep breath, she felt safe in Aaron's arms, but between her legs she felt a little tingle and the image of Brent popped into her head. Damn, why was she thinking about sex at a time like this?

After the funeral, Aaron, insisting that he go back to Finger Lakes with Jasmine was surprised when she said he should concentrate on getting the co-op ready to sell. She wanted to keep Aaron at bay so she could enjoy the wild fornicating with Brent and she decided to set the stage for a separation. "Well Aaron, I think it better that we stay away from one another for awhile. I am still upset with you about Brent. I don't want you trying to run my life. I think it better that we be away from each other for the immediate future."

Aaron, who had begun to question Jasmine's state of mind recently, said, "Denise called me Jasmine before she died. She seemed very concerned about something. She only left a message on my answering machine to call her. She was dead before I called, but I think I know what it was she wanted to discuss."

"And what was it?"

"My guess is that you are up in Finger Lakes with another man? I think you are cheating on me. I am a detective, and my instincts are pretty astute. Tell me the truth, who are you seeing?"

Jasmine, shocked at Aaron's perceptiveness, could only muster an "ah, ah, ah."

Aaron, now feeling deep pain growing within, said, "Is it one man or many?"

Jasmine, not wanting to reveal the truth of her tryst with Brent, said, "I have been on a few dates. I admit it. I am just seeing a few men for dinner; that is all."

Aaron, his heart sinking, as he could never have fathomed Jasmine doing this, replied "You're lying. It is Brent isn't it?"

Jasmine, feeling great trepidation that she had been caught in her lie, stammered out, "O.K., yes it is Brent. It is he. I admit it. There is the truth. I am in love with him!"

Aaron had never felt pain like he was experiencing at that moment. Wounded in Vietnam, overwhelmed with grief when his grandmother died, watching his father and mother pass away from the debilitating effects of emphysema had not been as profound. This was a blow he simply could not comprehend, because he genuinely believed that this woman had such a deep, abiding love for him that she was beyond reproach when it came to fidelity. He believed that he was so dearly loved by this woman that no man could win her heart, because Aaron was her protector, her knight in shining armour who had saved her from despair and the certain death promised by the assassin, the *Whirlwind*. He had foolishly believed her when she professed undying fealty and love so many times. He believed in her and believed in their devotion to one another.

This strong man wilted into tears, as he stood there in disbelief, weeping like a baby as the reality of the situation penetrated his heart like a hot lance probing into his flesh, twisting, turning and destroying his insides as he faced the reality of a situation that was simply beyond the realm of possibility in his mind that had never even entertained the thought that this woman could seek the arms of another man. He was old, losing his hair, developing a pot-belly, had seen his libido diminish appreciably, and his depression was sometimes intolerable, but he believed that his devotion to her was enough to sustain their marriage. He had foolishly thought that was enough for a woman who had always looked up to him as not only a husband, but also a father figure who was her protector. Aaron felt so betrayed, because he was not able to see that it was his own actions that contributed to what was now a crisis of the heart, mind and soul. Aaron was a defeated man. Yes, he was now a dead man walking!

Having endured what she thought was the unendurable; Jasmine simply had no emotions left when it came to Aaron. She stood stoically and proclaimed in one statement that which would haunt Aaron's mind until he took his last breath, "Stop the crying. We have played out. You will never put your tongue down my throat again. Leave me alone and go back home and find someone else. We are through."

At that moment, Aaron fell to his knees, weeping uncontrollably. This strong man who had endured war, battled against assassins, fought vile corruptness on the streets of despair, lived in the underbelly of a society with no justice, survived brutal physical beatings in a profession that offered more despair than hope, lay nearly prostrate as be begged her not to leave him.

Finally, a small modicum of emotion seemed to emanate from Jasmine as she said, "O.K., O.K., I still love you, but not the way you want. I will always love you, because I know you are my protector, the man who lifted me up when I was so low I thought I could never climb up from the pit of despair that engulfed me, the man who has always been there when I needed him. You are, after all, the man who saved me from the *Whirlwind*. How can I ever forget that? I wouldn't be alive today if it wasn't for you. Stop the crying, stop the pleading; I will always look after you. I owe you that much, but I will no longer sleep in your bed; share your hopes, desires and dreams. That is finished."

Aaron, the strong man who had stood against overwhelming odds so often in his life, rose and said, "I will accept any indignity to be with you – any indignity. I have no life without you. I am nothing without you – nothing."

Jasmine, still stoic and methodically clinical in her manner, but feeling a tinge of compassion for a man she had never seen so vulnerable, said, "You are not going to like what you are going to get, but if you want this type life, then you are welcome in my at my house, but as a guest, not a husband. I will usher you through this painful period and try to show you some understanding and compassion, but I say again, you will not like it. You Aaron are destined to pay a price you may not be willing to pay."

ESCAPE THE DARKNESS

It was there for all to see.
She made Aaron all he could be.
Investing his life in love,
He believed she was sent from heaven above.

The darkness brought by her desertion
Could only lead Aaron to one assertion.
She would one day raise the alarm,
And ask again his protection from harm.

Her slights of affection made him wonder
If she had forgotten all and tossed love asunder.
Yet, he sensed that her love was still there,
But it lived in a heart that was no longer fair.

Would he ever again share her bed?
Oh, what could ameliorate the horrible dread?
Was all the good he had done to be disposed
In acrimonious disregard as her chamber closed?

Like a roller-coaster dipping up and down
He longed for that old love to be found.
He would absolutely hold nothing in reserve.
It was she he still wanted to serve.

His light was low and dim.
She cast him aside on a nefarious whim.
Still his love would grow greater each day,
Until, in his grave he would lay.

The Girl Who Motivated Murder Most Foul

Still her champion, he would not bend in the wind,
No matter how much he was chagrined.
Hope springs eternal in his emptiness,
That she will let him escape the darkness.

.

To her he was less than the cloud to the wind,
To her he was less than the foam to the sea,
To her he was less than the rose to the storm
Remorsefulness for his slights she could not see.

But to him she was brighter than the stars at night,
She was more than the rain to the lea,
She was more than heaven to the earth
To his broken heart, she held the key.

Darkness descended on Aaron as he watched Jasmine leave for Finger Lakes. For the first time in 20 years, he was truly alone. He would beg, plead and cajole, all to no avail. He was about to descend into a deep, dark abyss of despair, and as he was doing so, in the back of his mind, he kept telling himself that there was something strange about Denise's demise. What was she doing out on the cliff by herself early in the morning, and why had she called him? Was it just because she wanted to tell him about Jasmine's affair, or was it because she knew something more sinister was at play? Yes, Aaron was naturally suspicious. It was the nature of his profession, but there was more to it than that. There was an element about Brent that simply caused him concern, and it went beyond a dislike just because he had stolen his wife. This was a man possessed of evil. He sensed it from the very beginning. Yeah, he was a man who hated those who did not conform to the defined patterns of society. He would have hated Denise. Would he have hated her enough to commit murder?

CHAPTER 4
TO ALWAYS CATCH YOU

The grimness of the grave
cannot hold the truth in abeyance.
The truth will from its trap escape.
It will look upon the sullen world
to see the lies and deceit.
But alas, Aaron is the seeker of truth.
He is a breath, a wind,
a shadow, a phantom.
Long shall he pursue truth,
undeterred by the mountain of lies
that are laid before him.
In the sweet bye and bye,
He who is indeed pure of heart.
Shall know truth's sanctity.

Thus began a period of deep reflection and intense loneliness for Aaron as he sent Jasmine a series of e-mails pleading with her to reconsider, to please give him an opportunity to win her back. As he tried to work, thoughts of her kept him immersed in his misery and prevented him from doing his job. What follows are some of the e-mails that reflect Aaron's slide into deep despair and hopelessness.

November 3: Jasmine, I have spent a restless night just staring at the walls. You are in love with another man and the wonderful life you think that he offers you. You wrap yourself in his arms and worship him, and I do nothing but pine for you while you dismiss me with disgust. I am so damn stupid. I hate myself for being a weakling but I am a prisoner of love for you. Just please don't completely desert me. Please!!!! Abuse and use me anyway you want, but please don't desert me. I hurt so much for that which I cannot have. I walked through the house several times last night looking at the empty spots where some of your things used to be, and I ached in solitude realizing many of your things rest elsewhere now. If you could experience my pain for 1 hour, you would realize how much I love you and say, "I can never get that much love from Brent. Aaron is worth a gamble just one time."

I am lower now than the day you admitted to an affair with Brent. I never thought any pain could be worse than that, but it just doesn't get better. It gets worse with each passing day, especially since you began completely ignoring me. Now, another weekend will see me bowing before the altar of misery as you frolic in blissfulness enjoying a life of domestic pleasure. PLEASE HAVE SOME COMPASSION FOR ME AND DON'T LEAVE ME TO FACE THE WORLD COMPLETELY WITHOUT YOU. You made so many promises about always taking care of me, but your love of that man grows stronger each day and those promises become meaningless to you. I know you will ignore this e-mail like you do all my e-mails, but please know I am lower than I ever imagined possible. I love you more than the breath of life itself.

November 4: I actually had hope long ago but that hope is Gone With The Wind now that you have practically moved in with him and embraced your new life with gusto. I love you Jasmine, and wish I could arise from the pain, but all I can do is say I love you, and if the time ever comes when you finally realize how much better off you would be with me, I am here to embrace you with more love than any man ever had for a woman. You detest me, but maybe one day you will look about you and analyze where you are and where you are headed, and realize that you could love me again as you once did if you gave hope and promise a chance. I live each day in anticipation of you gracing our co-op once again so that it becomes a home once more. You are the sunshine that lights up my darkness. I am here to make your life all it should be if given the chance. I screwed it up the first time. I would never make that mistake again.

November 5: I know you think this man offers you ambrosias utopia, but deep within my heart I sense that you still have time to think of me just a little. I have no one here. There is no place in my heart for anyone but you. Anyone who enters my world is only on a transitory journey through my misery to assuage the loneliness of my existence for a brief period. I can work magic bringing hope to so many as I reach out with compassion to those who are adrift in a sea of agony and lost hope. How ironic that I can offer hope to others, but I have no hope for myself.

November 6: Each weekend without you I know takes you further and further from me as you embrace he whom you love so much now. I am so empty and flounder in loneliness for that which made my life worthwhile. I know you have discarded me permanently, but I cannot help but love you deeply still, because I cannot break from that love which will forever bind my heart to you. I wish you could feel my pain for just an hour, and you would know that no man can ever love you as I do, no matter how much you are coaxed and beguiled. I long for you more now than ever before, because each day as you turn ever further from me, I, on the other hand, embrace my love for you as I never have before. Love hurts, but it is a hurt I gladly bare for having had you for the time I did.

November 7: I could not help but think of you tonight as I do every night in lonely silence. I keep asking myself how I could have been so lucky to have you for 20 years and so unlucky to drive you away. There are times when I pine for your company and I know you are asleep with he has your love now, so I look at some of your pictures and that radiant smile fills the hole in my heart with memories that cascade through my mind like gentle water babbling in a stream. You are the pot of gold at the end of the rainbow, Jasmine, for any man lucky enough to have you. The greatest treasures are invisible to the eye, but they are found by the heart. I am so glad my heart found its greatest treasure for 20 years. Thank you for those 20 years that I look upon now with longing. I no longer have the treasure, but memories linger and shall always remind me of what I have lost.

It get's cold early in Finger Lakes, so Jasmine came to the city to pick up some things from the co-op, and she and Aaron had lunch that day. As they sat in the restaurant, Aaron gazed upon her loveliness and with a tears in his eyes, he said, "My life has been reduced to waiting. Yes, waiting for those one or two e-mails each day. You are physically only a short distance from me, but you are emotionally in your heart now a world away. How, I ask myself can an old man who has been abandoned still love so dearly she who quickens my pulse and makes my heart beat with the rhythm of attachment, devotion, ardour and frenzied excitement. You are a golden tear I shed each day in contemplative reflection of a life that was filled with the gracious unselfish kindness of she who brings a twinkle to my eye, she who reaches into the depths of my soul to shine a beacon of light into the darkness, she who once kissed my loneliness away with moist, wet, succulent lips of passion. I gaze upon that angelic face that graces our home in photos and can see the affection you once had for me floating like a vapour in the humid summer air. I want to amorously devour not just your body, but your soul. I want to worship at your altar of love, embracing your kindness, courtesy, unselfishness and benevolent tenderness. You are the raging fire that sears my soul and burns away despair. Oh, how I love you. Oh, how I lament what I have lost and I pine for you in the darkness of my despair. I love you more Jazzy with each passing day. The ardour, the love, the devotion I might receive from anyone else is meaningless in the scheme of things, because my heart is broken and can never be mended by another. It can only be bandaged for a moment in time until the wound is opened again and the pain returns with even more intensity. Holidays are exercises in desperation as I imagine you frolicking in joy while misery surrounds me. The idea of seeing you on occasion is all that sustains me. It makes me continue breathing in the hope that I will be graced with your presence and once again bask in the radiance which once shined upon only me."

Jasmine, seemingly perturbed, said, "Aaron get over it. I told you that you and I have simply played out. I am in love with a wonderful, kind, loving man now who makes me feel so alive and vibrant."

Aaron lowered his head, almost as if in shame for loving her so much. "I hope you are joking. You lie in bed with him every night, you fawn over him like he was a God of love, you caress him, you tell him how much you love him, and you take care of him and his sexual needs. You allow him to control you like he is a potentate of love as you dutifully jump like a servant to gaze upon his smiley faces of manipulation sent on that dastardly cell-phone he gave you to keep tabs on you. You willingly bow to his restrictive domination. You let him abuse you with contemptuous disrespect for your value as a woman all the while as I am still wallowing in the misery of regret because I am discarded and tossed into the valley of despair because all my adulation is forgotten as you bow before the altar of he who is not worthy to lay on the ground and have you walk over him with contemptuous disregard."

Aaron sighed and continued. "This is a man who said he was going to take care of you. He is the man who is going to buy you a home, a car, a ticket to the paradise of his love. This is the man who tells you to quit work and he will lay before you a golden path of harmonious contentment in the valley of amorous adulation that is nothing more than the screens and mirrors of a magician of restrictive containment of your free spirit that should soar to the heavens of possibility and promise, not be corralled by the regimented domination of a man who is too stupid to realize what he has. I know what you are. You are the sun that greets each day with a golden radiance. You are the warm air of the afternoon that heats up the heart of he who adores you from afar now. You are the moon that glows at night and shines a light of serenity and peace on he who is lucky enough to lie beside you and feel the delights of flesh that is warm and inviting. While he whom you make your God of love eviscerates, devitalizes and weakens your worth as a person and talks a game that he refuses to play, I am here to be your old dependable Aaron who never has and never will abandon you to the machinations of fools like this cretin who sees you as a possession to be locked up for his personal aggrandizement rather than as a woman who is to be given free reign in a kingdom that lies before her like the yellow brick road of happiness."

Shaking her said, all Jasmine could say was, "But I love him."

Aaron, perplexed at how such a refined, gentle, kind woman could love such a man could only put his head in his hands as he sit at the table perplexed and bewildered. He said very calmly, "I have done all I can to beg and plead for you to come home – to turn your back on this foolishness. I have kept my melancholia in check in front of you in hopes that you would see that I want to never do anything to displease you. You desert me and move in with another man, flaunt him in my face and tell me how much you love him and how much you detest me. Make me beg for attention and love, and somehow I am the ogre in your mind? I have always taken care of you and always will, but if you love this man so much and worship at his altar of foolish disregard for frugality, why do you not put demands on him? You proudly proclaim him as your lover for the entire world to see and shame me to the world as a fool who still humbly bows before you like a slave of love. Please don't be this way to me. I thought you still cared for me just a little. I thought that you might one day realize that I am here waiting for your return to where you belong. Stop and think long and hard. I know my foolishness contributed to driving you into another man's arms. He degrades you daily and you still long to be by his side when he mouths another apology for heinous behaviour that he will continue. I will never act in the foolish fashion I did before. Give me the same chance you have given him. Pack your bags and come home where you belong. I know you still love me."

Jasmine glared at Aaron, but could muster no words as he continued. "I am going to get you what you want in life even when you are with another man. I have worked diligently in hopes that you would once again embrace me with affection and realize that you are better off with me than Brent. Please don't degrade he who has always worshipped and adored you. Pack you bags and come home, please. You will never regret it, because together we would still be a formidable team. Come on darling, you loved me once very deeply. You could learn to do it again. Come home to me please!"

Now, she struggled for words but they finally came. "Aaron, I do still love you, but I love him differently. I cannot explain it, but my hormones rage with excitement when I am around him. You see his missing teeth. You see his scraggily beard. You see his pot belly. You see his lack of hygiene. You see his uncouth manner. But I see the good in him, and I feel a fire between my legs that only he can put out."

Aaron was beginning to feel a rage building up, kept his temper under control. "You lie in bed with him every night, you fawn over him like he was a God of love, you caress him, you tell him how much you love him nad you take care of his sexual needs. You allow him to control you like he is a potentate of love as you dutifully jump like a servant to gaze upon his smiley faces of manipulation sent on that dastardly instrument of control and restrictive domination that he bought you. That cell phone is a ball and chain. You let him abuse you with contemptuous disrespect for your value as a woman all the while as I am still wallowing in the misery of regret, because I am discarded and tossed into the valley of despair as all my adulation is forgotten while you bow before the altar of he who is not worthy to lay on the ground and have you walk over him with contemptuous disregard."

Jasmine sit more erect in her seat and seemed to be actually mulling over what Aaron was saying as he continued. "This is a man who said he was going to take care of you. He is the man who is going to buy you a home, a car, a ticket to the paradise of his love. This is the man who tells you to quit work and he will lay before you a golden path of harmonious contentment in the valley of amorous adulation that is nothing more than the screens and mirrors of a magician of restrictive containment of your free spirit that should soar to the heavens of possibility and promise, not be corralled by the regimented domination of a man who is too stupid to realize what he has. I know what you are. You are the sun that greets each day with a golden radiance. You are the warm air of the afternoon that heats up the heart of he who adores you from afar now. You are the moon that glows at night and shines a light of serenity and peace on he who is lucky enough to lie beside you and feel the delights of flesh that is warm and inviting. While he whom you make your God of love eviscerates, devitalizes and weakens your worth as a person and talks a game that he refuses to play, I am here to be your old dependable Aaron who never has and never will abandon you to the machinations of fools like this man who sees you as a possession to be locked up for his personal aggrandizement rather than as a woman who is to be given free reign in a kingdom that lies before her like a golden treasure of happiness and contentment."

Aaron could see that she was giving deep thought to what he was saying, and he smiled while continuing, "Never underestimate your worth because that allows others to ignore your value. I will never underestimate your worth. And you should never fall for anyone who is not willing to catch you. I am here my sweet to always catch you!"

CHAPTER 5
HOW HE LONGED FOR HER

If I die tomorrow
tell it to the trees
how much I loved you.
Tell it to the soft breeze
that rustles leaves to the ground
that you are my world.
Tell it to the sky above
that I adore you.

Tell it to soft summer rain,
even it wouldn't understand.
Tell it to your cat,
whose meow reminds you
of how much you are loved by me.
Tell it to a wall made of stone,
shout it in the city streets
how much Aaron loves you.

But don't shout it too loud,
because people will not believe you.
It must be a whisper on the wind.
It must be a drop of morning dew.
No one could comprehend,
no one could possibly believe
that you are loved so much.
They simply could not understand
how one man could love one woman
so much, so much, so much.

There was a seed planted in Jasmine's mind that day she spent with Aaron – a seed of discontent with what she had decided to do with her life. Was she making the right decision? Was she allowing her hormones to dictate her actions rather than her mind? Was Aaron right about Brent? As she prepared to head back to Finger Lakes, she called Aaron and asked to meet for lunch again. Aaron, ever hopeful of her return to his arms, excitedly sat across from her and said, "I love you so much, but know it is too late to ameliorate that which has hardened your heart against me. I love you Jasmine and humbly beseech you to not turn your back on he who will spend the rest of his life suppliantly paying penance for any perceived sins against you. Please do not harden you heart against me."

Jasmine felt Aaron's love, but there was something inside her that refused to let go of the other man who had captured her heart. Deep inside she knew that Brent was anathema to that which was right and just, but she longed for his powerful thrusts into her body that sent waves of euphoric ecstasy cascading over her. "Aaron, I cannot help loving Brent."

Aaron, each time he heard her profess her love for that despicable man, felt as if an arrow had pierced his heart. He calmly said, "When you left me, a small piece of me died inside, and the deterioration of my mind, body and spirit continues toward oblivion. For 20 years you were the thread that kept my fragile psyche from tumbling over the precipice into the valley of permanent despair. Although I was always on that precipice and fighting against your desperate attempts to save me without realizing I was making you teeter over the abyss of misery along with me, I was at least kept above the darkness that waited for me. Now, the darkness embraces me. For all those years I was a contemptuous fool and did not realize the agony I was causing you. Now that I can see more clearly, it is too late to make recompense and rekindle the flame that burned so brightly in your heart for me all those years. How I long for that little girl who used to be filled with so much love that she would become overwhelmed with emotion when we had quarrels. She was that little girl who just wanted to be protected and corralled in the safety of my arms. My life now is utterly meaningless, because I do not have you by my side. It is as if the God of Revenge is playing a cruel hoax on me. I unknowingly sowed a wind of disdain in your heart, and I am now reaping the whirlwind of discontent. We have shared so much together. In spite of your antipathy toward me, I think you know that I was a guide who helped lead you through the maze of circumstances you faced because of your uniqueness. You once said,

'Enjoy the journey.' Oh, what a grand and glorious journey I have had with you. So regardless of how you feel about me, no nastiness or vileness can dissever the connection we have. We are connected and no matter what either of us does, I hope that connection will never be severed, because it is all I have left in a useless, meaningless existence."

Aaron bowed his head and simply contemplated on what he had lost:

> *You come to me a bit forlorn today.*
> *Oh, how I want to embrace you my dear.*
> *You had so much to sadly say.*
> *And I want to quiet your fear.*
>
> *Why can't you once again love me,*
> *When I've loved you for so long?*
> *Perhaps you could just try to see*
> *That I am part of your sweet song.*
>
> *I might bring smiles to fill your days,*
> *And words to fit your songs.*
> *If only you would come and stay.*
> *I've loved you for so long.*
>
> *Vainly, you search elsewhere to find*
> *The love you forever seek.*
> *Touch and take this love of mine,*
> *A love that's yours to keep.*

In deep thought, Aaron was snapped back to reality when Jasmine said, "I must go."

Aaron, almost pleading, said "I have done everything in my power to show you the folly of your obsession. You indicated to me that he said that he could not compete with me. What a laugh. It is I who cannot compete. I am not a master manipulator? I am a sheep duelling with a wolf! And you? You are a lamb in the wolf's den; afraid to free yourself for fear that it might offend the wolf and cause him to pounce upon you. Ironically, you cannot see that he has already devoured your mind and soul!"

Aaron was becoming more passionate now. "I have humbled myself and bowed to demeaning treatment to protect you from the harm you are determined to do to yourself. I ache deep within, because someone I love dearly refuses to see that which is so obvious. They say love is blind, but, in your case, it is also deaf and dumb. To reach you is impossible. Had I been given the opportunities this man has been given, I could have won you back. I have watched you turn a blind eye to two episodes of felonious actions on his part in less than six weeks. He cheated on you once already. You told me that you saw an e-mail to another woman wanting a date. He may not have met her, but if you had not caught him, he would have. Then, he went behind your back and told people at work that the two of you were engaged and warned other men to stay away from you when you picked him up at work. This man wants to own you! Those episodes of discontent should have shown the depth of depravation to which you have submitted yourself. Yet, through it all you crawl in supplication, forgiving that which, in my case, you would never forgive. My transgressions never included the pursuit of another woman! I ache inside for you, as I see you throw away your life for love that is shallow and offers nothing concrete and lasting, but rather offers turmoil, subservience to an ogre who presents a façade of deceit and fosters ambiguities of intent."

For the first time, Aaron was being forceful with her as he continued. "The disdain I have received from you is well-deserved perhaps, but it has not made my commitment to you falter. I know that real love is not just mouthing the words or buying frivolous gifts. Love is proved through positive actions that may not generate instant gratification, but assures a life where gratification will be there in old age. This man has never had a frugal day in his life, which is why he is almost 50 years old and has nothing. He lives for the moment with complete disregard for what may lie ahead."

"This man wins even when he loses, because you are trapped in his Svengali web of deceit, control and manipulation. The flirtatious episode was only the tip of the iceberg. It should have been the final blow in an episodic display of malicious intentions. Yet, all is forgiven for love. You are like a 20 year old little girl, trapped at home with her parents, desperate to replace that which she thinks is unendurable. If you must replace the unendurable, then at least explore what is out there and do not just settle. You are still young, vital, intelligent and capable of great things. You look for any excuse to supplicate yourself to a life of desperation in the arms of this man. Do not supplicate yourself for that which will drag you into an abyss of despair and trap you in a life of desperation and eventual bankruptcy financially and emotionally. I said I would always be there to protect you, and I have done my best, but you have exhausted me and he has defeated me. I lie bloodied on a battlefield where even my honour was sacrificed in your defence. My defeat is total and irrevocable. He stands victorious, because, like the Trojan horse, he has nefariously gotten inside the walls of your heart and mind. He has stealthily crept into the heart and soul of the one I love. So complete is his control of you that he has enlisted you in the destruction of me, whom you still profess to have feelings for. His hatred of me borders on the psychotic, because he knows that once you are free of me, his control is complete and you cannot escape his grasp. I was all that stood between him and his conquest of your mind, body and soul. His victory is complete.

You will submit to any degradation to wrap yourself in his hairy arms of manipulation and control. I ache for you! I cry for you! I suffer agony and despair for you! Yet, it is all in vain, because you are so determined to destroy a life of great hope and possibility for that which will degrade, belittle and trap you. You have more opportunity and more hope than 90% of the women in the world, and I had a lot to do with making things that way, because rather than filling your ears with false manipulative *I love you's*, I spent the last 20 years proving my love by giving you security and hope for a future free of want. I am no saint, but I am the man who was and always will be devoted to your welfare, regardless of your shameful disregard for my feelings and the things I have done for you. I will not forsake you now, tomorrow or as long as I have breath. In fact, even without breath, when I am ashes scattered to the winds, my spirit, through the things I have arranged for you, will still be there, trying to keep you safe from harm, despite your own malfeasance. Love? No one you are with now or in the future will ever display the depth of love I have for you. It is eternal and everlasting. It knows no boundaries, not even death!"

There was a time when Aaron could have reached her, but it was no longer possible. Emotions within her had seemed to wither and die except in relation to Brent. She looked at Aaron as if he were some creature that had risen from the foul depths of the hell. "I have heard enough of your disparaging tirade attacking he whom I love."

She reached down, picked up her beautiful red scarf that Aaron had bought her long ago. Aaron looked at it as she wrapped it around her neck and felt the deepest discontent of his life.

My life is now like a book filled with tragedy.
I read over and over hoping for a happy ending.
Trees of fall lie at angles in my mind,
felled by a winter storm of discontent,
and she whom I love prepares for the
cold weather far from me in the arms of another.

November light slants through the oaks of my mind
as a parade of lost hope passes in my psyche,
shushing with the winter wind searching treetops
for the last leaf to steal from the tree of life.
Love lies on a forest floor, not evergreen but oaken,
its branches latched to a greying sky as I die.
Yes, as I die from the heartache!

Now her winter scarf is gone with her,
and in its place she left a scathing bookmark.
It is a mark that says she will never return
to explore what we knew and did not know.
Oh, we knew once in the spreading twilight
love that is now a flowing scarf of discontent
for me who is left in loneliness and despair.

Neither of them said anything as she walked out, leaving Aaron sighing in disbelief that he was unable to reach her. He got up, paid the bill and strolled into the teeming streets of Manhattan, but he was more alone than he had ever been in his life.

It was about two o'clock. Aaron simply could not do it. He could not go into his dank little office. He continued to walk. He headed to uptown Manhattan, where the smart set was taking their lunch break. He noticed how gaily and lightly people he passed carried their radiant heads, and swung themselves through life as through it was a ball-room. There was no sorrow in a single look he met, no burden on any shoulder, perhaps not even a clouded thought, not a little hidden pain in any of the happy souls. Aaron hugged those thoughts as he continued his journey to nowhere. Insignificant incidents, miserable details of perceived slights by Jasmine and her lack of love for him forced their way into his imagination and scattered about in a hopeless torrent of despair that wracked his brain.

It was as if some phantom were following him, whisking about overhead as a ghostly apparition. Why had the hand of fate turned against him? Why against him? Was not he a kind, generous and loving person? Why did he suffer this agony deep within his soul?

He asked himself if he was paying for all the individuals he had targeted for assassination when he was an intelligence analyst in the army? Or was it for the two people he had killed that night in a firefight to escape certain death? From the time he was a little boy, he felt ill-luck was his destiny. He could clearly notice he was gradually increasing debilities; he had become too languid to control or lead himself from the dark pit into which he was falling. He felt like someone had bored a way into his soul and hollowed him out. There was only emptiness.

Was he intended for annihilation like the people he had targeted for assassination? His whole being was at that moment in the highest degree of torture. He felt the weight of an anvil pressing down upon his shoulders. The people who came and went around him glided past like faint gleams of light. He strolled toward Central Park where he found seat by the duck pond.

Aaron wished he believed in God, because only a God could assuage his despair. He felt as if his brains were spilling out of his head, leaving a deep, dark, empty vacuum. Damn he thought to himself. Damn this despair that envelopes me and embraces my soul.

He grew bitterer about his afflictions of despair. Why were obstacles to happiness always put between him and that which he should have? He looked up towards the sky and cursed his fate.

Everything around him was suddenly a distraction. Gnats were flittering all about and he brushed them away with a flick of the hand. He let his eyes glide down to his chest and noticed he was breathing heavily. His gaze continued downward and he noticed the jerking movement his foot made each time his heart beat. Suddenly a feeling of recognition trembled through his senses; the tears welled up in his eyes, and a soft voice seemed to whisper – "you are weak. You are weak!" He closed his eyes and the physical tears dried up, but inside he was bawling with sorrow.

A small man sat on the bench with him, and unfolded a newspaper. The insane idea entered Aaron's head that it might be a quite particular newspaper, even unique. His curiosity increased, and he began to move backwards and forwards on the seat. It might be dangerous documents about a conspiracy as sinister as 9/11.

The man sat quietly and pondered over his newspaper. On the far side, near the armrest of the bench, was a small brown package with a white string tied around it. Aaron began to wonder what was in it. Was it a bomb? No, Aaron's mind was just playing tricks on him. Watching Jasmine leave was just too much – too much.

He thought about going home, but knew he couldn't. No, it was no longer a home without Jasmine. It was a dark, dank, miserable tomb now. There were simply too many reminders of her there, and the silence of the place had become almost deafening.

IN SILENCE

Where once the sounds of lovers' hearts pounded
Now sit silent and empty rooms.
The oak floors creak as if embracing loneliness.
Wishful thoughts of a rumbled bed
Ah, midnight fantasies in my head.

In frenzied haste our clothes we would shed.
Sweet memories, but alas there is now silence.
The gaiety is gone with broken pieces of hearts.
Paths cross now and then, but our time is gone.
She says love dissipated, so I am alone.

We had our time in glorious euphoria,
But now there is silence.
How can storied silence be so painful,
And so infernally deafening?
The season of our discontent descended
upon us in a cloud,
As the time of radiant blooming
passed into winter frost.
In between, lived happiness,
but now in silence it is lost.

Exiting the park, Aaron noticed the wind was picking up. Aaron thought to himself "was there a hole to be found where he could creep in and hide himself from life?" Visions; senseless dreams!

The day seemed to race away as the great spirit of darkness spread a shroud over Aaron. Everything was silent--everything. But there was a symphony of symbols playing in Aaron's head, no, not a symphony, a funeral dirge. He shuffled off toward home in the gloom and agony of despair. When would it end?

Fury welled up in Aaron, blazing with brutal strength. He was becoming mentally and physically more and more unstable. Each day, he sank deeper into the morass of despair.

In the dark abyss of the mind, angry demons bristle with range to make the pain unbearable. Aaron placed his hands over his ears, left the co-op and began walking. He quickened his pace, almost fearing that some unknown beast was stalking him.

He was now desperately dragging one foot after the other. He felt a scorching heat in his head, and his temples pulsated. He rounded a corner, stepped into the alley and threw up, heaving vast quantities of green matter that fell at his feet. He was sick, so sick.

The Girl Who Motivated Murder Most Foul

He felt a gnawing in his chest, so he sat down on a bus bench, exhausted as he put his elbows on his knees and his head in his hands. He sat for a long time as the wind blew lustily through the chestnut trees around him, and the day began to decline into darkness.

He walked up and down the street not going in any particular direction. The wind freshened, the clouds chased madly across the sky dancing in joyful merriment, and they gradually disappeared as it got darker. He walked, and began to cry for no reason. An hour passed; passed with such strange slowness, such weariness.

The day began to decline, the sun sank and a slight breeze rustled the leaves on the trees. Aaron closed his eyes, and got more and more sleepy. He sat down on a bench and gradually dozed off, but sprang immediately up, realizing it was getting late. He had wasted a day.

Aaron felt himself like a creeping thing on the verge of destruction, gripped by ruin in the midst of a whole world ready for lethargic sleep. He was oppressed by weird terrors, and took some furious strides down the path out of the park as he said to himself, "Enough of this melancholia."

All through the night until the bright dawn Aaron walked the streets in despair. He felt his life ebbing away. There was emptiness deep within him, and he was untouched by all around him. He had descended into his own little world. He sat down and put his feet up on the seat and leaned back. He felt isolated and alone. Only the lonely, crooning voice of silence struck in monotones on his ears, and the lurking monsters of despair in his mind drew him into a cocoon of darkness. His thoughts raced like a hurricane coming ashore in the gulf. He stumbled down the street.

He promised to the darkness around him that he would pull himself out of it, make himself whole again. Some remedy for his predicament would turn up!

He stumbled on, as he wept silently with emotion. Suddenly he thought of his dear friend Bruce, the one man who would have an understanding of his pain, because he had been in so much despair himself but had risen from the depth of darkness to find light. Yes, he would find Bruce.

He lived far away, but he could make it. He knew he could. Aaron struggled toward Bruce's apartment building. When he got there he just stood and stared at it. He told himself that had he become loathsome, and he did not want Bruce to see him in that condition. He turned and headed back up the street, keeping his eyes on lamppost after lamppost, steadily moving onward, but to where? Was he walking to his doom?

Suddenly Aaron's knees trembled fearfully, and he stopped to support himself against a lamppost. Filling with determination, he started once again putting one foot in front of another but going where?

The agony of Aaron continued unabated as he felt a sickening emptiness inside, but he could not go in supplication to his beloved Jasmine and beg her to wrap her arms around him and take him back into her warm bosom of hope. He did not want her to see him as a weak old man with no hope. She deserved better.

He finally made it home, lay on the sofa and the room began to whirl about in his mind and he recalled the interludes of lovemaking with Jasmine that had been so exciting. Before Jasmine he had only existed, not lived. Ah, sweet love. The years flowed by in his mind as he lay there contemplating what he had lost.

Tonight I lie here thinking of what I had.
Oh, the thought you are gone makes me so sad.
I treasured you, never treated you as a possession,
But was there within me some secret aggression.
If only you had known that you were treasured,
And that every step I took was precisely measured.

The Girl Who Motivated Murder Most Foul

I guess without knowing it I pushed you away.
Yes, I made colossal miscalculations every day.
Too often I spoke in haste and with anger.
I placed your fragile heart in danger.
I never realized that you had corralled your love,
As you just waited for me to make the final shove.
My inner turmoil boiled with frustration,
But for you I still had great admiration.
Oh, how I wish I could kiss you again with care.
You are my life, my hope, my promise dear.
I should have treasured each day.
I was stupid. What else can I say?

He rolled over on his side and stared at the far wall where a picture of he and Jasmine hung on the wall. Tears formed in his eyes and he began to sob. How he longed for her!

CHAPTER 6
HOTTER THAN THE FIRES OF HELL

My love sleeps far from me now.
Her heart and soul are at peace.
Ah, how she is dearly loved by me.
She is more beautiful than
any work of art ever produced,
because no painting by any artist,
no stroke of the brush
can adequately capture such beauty.

Silence fills the walls of my room,
and the night is calm but lonely,
as my thoughts are like the trees
taking deep root into the earth of my soul.
Towering mountains and the stars
that shine above them
rise into an endless
tribute to she who sleeps.

I wonder in her dreams
if places from our past she sees,
and maybe she has some memories of
the faces, events and joys we shared.
I am moved and elevated
by her quiet outer and inner beauty
that dwells deep within my heart.
Ah, my love sleeps but my affection never rests.

When the night has come

and the land is covered in darkness,
when the moon is the only light there is,
look at its brightness in the heavens
and you can sense the glowing intensity
of my deep abiding love for her.

Thus was Aaron in the throes of misery pining for Jasmine and his mind was slowly deteriorating, slowly free-falling toward oblivion. Could he defeat the depression that was overwhelming him?

Can you not minister to a mind diseased?
Pluck from the memory a rooted sorrow,
Raze out the written troubles of the brain,
And with some sweet oblivious antidote
Cleanse the heavy heart of that perilous stuff
which weighs upon the soul?
Sometimes the answer is no,
and it is then that the mind goes into free-fall
and drops into the abyss of despair.

That night Aaron's mind was free-falling into a private hell as the enormity of his loss overwhelmed him. He tossed about the sofa and moaned in misery, as if he had suffered a fatal physical blow that had opened up an untreatable wound. The blood was flowing profusely from his wounded heart as his life poured out in an endless stream of memories cast forever in the far reaches of his mind to be treasured, savored and recalled with delight for that which was now gone.

Sex is as powerful an element as the atom. It can explode with a fury that captures the soul in a cascading search for euphoria that soars upwards into the far reaches of the mental universe in search of nirvana. As the morning sun peeped in through the blinds, Aaron blinked to avoid the glare and thought about how sex had been such an intricate part of his life. He reflected back on one of his greatest conquests – the first time he had sex with B.J., his secretary, whom he loved dearly, but who had been lost in the famous case of the mysterious box as told by his biographer in the best-selling *Fall from Apocalypse*.

B.J. urged him to get undressed and join her in bed. He instantly complied, and she commenced undressing as she lay on the bed. Every detail of her charming body devoured his greedy eyes. Her smooth, glossy, and abundant hair that cascaded down to her shoulders touched the tips of her nipples. She looked divine. She reached out with both her arms as she spread her legs and enticed him to get on top of her so she could feel his warmth.

She whispered, "Place yourself on your knees between my out-spread thighs - there, that is it darling - now let me lay hold of your dear instrument and guide it into my warm wetness that craves your manliness. Oh, how I have longed to have your love muscle plunge into me."

He placed himself on her beautiful smooth and silken belly and pressed against the hair of her mound. With her long tapering fingers, she guided him into the opening to the gates of heaven. Aaron trembled in every limb and almost felt sick with excitement - but when he felt the delicious sensation caused by the insertion of his member into the smooth warm oily folds of her mound of desire, he gave but one shove which carried him deep within her so that he actually swooned with delight.

When he exploded in her, he laid on her, breathing heavily, his member still sheathed into her warmth. B.J. rhythmically squeezed his love muscle with gyrations inside her opening. Suddenly, he was throbbing in the most ecstatic way as she was pressing and closing with every fold on his swelling member - which had hardly lost any of its pristine stiffness; as his eyes began to discern her features, an exquisite smile played upon his darling companion's lips. She was being devilish and enjoying it immensely.

She pushed Aaron off her and smiled as she turned over on her stomach and said, "This is what your really want. I know it. A real man like you feels more powerful when you are pounding a woman in her most intimate part. Go ahead baby. Go ahead and take that which will bring you the greatest of pleasure."

His hands found their way to her large plump smooth bottom. He was in a rampant state, and at once began forcing his throbbing member between the delicious cheeks of her immense bottom as she turned on her side. He wanted his member sheathed in her tightness. Aaron pressed stoutly forward against her luscious body, knowing that the entrance to the temple of pleasure was eagerly awaiting his thrusts. He found more difficulties than he expected, but at length began to penetrate, although the orifice appeared much tighter than he expected. Excited by the difficulties of entrance, he clasped the lady firmly round the waist and pushed forcibly and steadily forward. He felt the folds give way to his iron stiffness, and one-half of it was fairly embedded in the extremely tight sheath. A convulsive pleasure of the sphincter caused him such exquisite satisfaction by the pressure of the folds on the more sensitive upper half of his member, which was so delicious, and so much tighter, and more exciting he could not resist the temptation of moaning with delight. He reached around and placed two fingers into her other orifice, and pressed his belly forwards with all his might. She moaned and he felt her body go limp as he ploughed ever forward much to her delight.

Afterward, they clasped each other in a most enrapturing embrace, and then B.J. allowed him to turn her in every direction so as to see, admire, and devour every charm of her exquisitely formed body. They caressed each other with such mutual satisfaction that nature soon drove them to a closer and more active union of the bodies.

Aaron suddenly shook his head as he lay on the sofa thinking of the conquest of B.J. and recalled that his real love was Jasmine, not her. How could he be thinking of another woman besides Jasmine? Could it be that he was beginning to fathom the idea of life without her?

Jasmine had ignored him for two entire days now. He was a burden to her, an anvil around her neck that she wanted to cut lose and be free of. While she was lying in her new lover's arms, Aaron thought to himself, "I am lying in a grave of sorrow."

Aaron's gun was lying on the coffee table. He lifted up the gun from the table and almost lovingly fondled it in his hand, embracing it like it was a miracle cure for his current situation. Every day he told himself that he would get hold of his emotions and win her back. Every night, as he was falling asleep and bawling like a baby, he would tell himself that he could get her back, and, thereby, end the pain.

One day without hearing her voice brought him to the brink of insanity. How he longed for one magical touch from her that might in some small way assuage the heartache.

He sighed; relaxed his grip on the gun and it fell to the floor with the barrel facing Aaron. He looked down at the barrel and saw it as a long tunnel that was luring him into darkness, because there was no longer any light in his life.

His mind, for so long, had held the weapon of deceit deep within, not wanting to face the fact that she whom he loved so much had practiced vile deception while fornicating with another man. Forth from this vine of malice spread the evil fruit. The earth trembled from the wound she inflicted upon the one who loved her so. Rising from his mental darkness, Aaron got up from the sofa and prepared to face oblivion.

He reached down, picked up his gun and placed it on the coffee table. A knock at the door seemed an annoyance, but he meandered down the hallway to open it and there stood his neighbour Charlene Nuemann. She was a fine example of womanhood thought Aaron as she stood there smiling at him. In her husky voice she said, "Aaron, I heard that Jasmine has left you. I am so sorry." As she talked, she slowly walked through the doorway without being asked. She actually walked past Aaron toward the living room, and Aaron observed the provocative sway of her magnificent hips as the tight fitting silk dress hugged every luscious curve like it had been painted on her skin. Aaron felt a tinkling sensation between his legs as he followed her and said, "Would you like a cup of coffee Charlene?"

A provocative, alluring smile slowly crept across her succulent, thick, luscious lips as she almost whispered, "I would be delighted." She then reached out and pulled Aaron toward her. She threw her arms round his neck, and drew him to her lips and gave him a sweet lingering kiss, which he returned with eagerness. He felt his member raise itself up to its full extent as the caresses were exchanged, and Charlene held him tightly pressed against her body and felt his huge member throbbing against her as she continued the conversation. "My, my, I think I can help you forget some of your troubles."

She dropped to her knees and began to unzip Aaron's pants as she said, "I have desired to do this for so long Aaron, but would never have wanted to come between you and Jasmine. However, now is my chance to taste the delights of a man I find extremely attractive."

It popped out at full-staff, almost slapping her in the face with its hardness. Delighted with its size, she smiled and devoured it in one gulp as Aaron moaned.

The Girl Who Motivated Murder Most Foul

Just as Aaron was about to explode his passion in her mouth, she eased off, looked up and said, "I am going to make you forget her at least for a little while. Get ready for the fuck of your life Aaron!"

Could Aaron forget for awhile? Was it possible? He looked at Charlene's loveliness as she stood and quickly pulled her dress over her head, revealing an underwear-less body that glistened in the bright sunlight showing little beads of sweet forming on her alabaster skin. Aaron liked dark-skinned women, but this time he would make an exception as he decided to cast caution to the wind and embrace this incredible opportunity to explore carnal delights with a young, nubile woman who was seething with sexual energy. Damn, he would put Jasmine out of his mind by wrapping himself in the arms of a creature of erotic delights. She had done it with someone else. Hell, she was probably doing it right then he thought. Yeah, she was wrapping herself in that disgusting man's hairy arms at that very moment!

Aaron undressed and the two strolled to the bedroom where Aaron and Jasmine had made love so many times. "Yeah," thought Aaron, but that is over. Jasmine is finished with me. I'll show her that two can play at the game. I may be old, but I can still get it up, and here is a young woman who really wants me. I am tired of wallowing in self-pity."

Charlene did not resist, she let Aaron do as he liked. Pushing himself down on her, he applied his lips and tongue to her lovely hairy opening, all wet with her discharge, which was so sweet to the taste that he first began licking between the lips, and then applied himself to her excited opening to paradise, and with his finger and thumb working frantically, threw her into an ecstasy of delight, until again she had a deliciously roaring discharge. Then creeping up, he thrust his huge member into her well-moistened and velvety opening.

"Stop, Aaron, darling, I will show you another position, where you can lie easily with your dear delightful stiffness up to the hilt in the sheath you have so charmingly excited. Here, lie down by my right side on your side. This is going to be so good!"

She lay down on her back, and throwing her right leg over his hips, told him to bend his knees forward and open his legs, and lift up her right leg. She placed her left thigh between his thighs and then slightly twisting her bottom up towards him brought the lips of her hairy mound directly before his stiff member, which she seized with her delicate fingers, and guided safely into her grotto of pleasure. "And now," she said, almost as if she was a teacher and Aaron was her willing young pupil, "shove hard, baby – real hard. I want to feel all your energy behind each thrust.

The Girl Who Motivated Murder Most Foul

As Aaron thrust violently into her, he took a mouth full of her delicious breasts, alternating between them as he whispered to her, "wouldn't want one tit to get jealous of all the attention the other is getting."

They had a good laugh and enjoyed a full morning of delightful sexual activity. Aaron, feeling young and vibrant again had managed to put his misery out of his mind for just awhile thanks to the kindness of Charlene. Some would call her a wanton whore thought Aaron, but I would call her an angel of kindness who saw an old man suffering and decided to bring him some joy. This was a kind and generous woman.

Day after day Aaron strove at his work in an attempt to get his mind off his worries, and each day the delightful Charlene came by his co-op to relieve his loneliness. Yet, the hole in his heart would not heal, and as he was fighting desperately to conquer his misery, other elements were playing out that were going to create even more turmoil as Brent sat with his brother and father, contemplating murder most foul. Yes, they were about to make murder a family affair.

Brent knew that if he was too have Jasmine, he would have to devise a means of getting Aaron completely out of her life as she was still too dependent on him for counsel.

His brother, puffing on a joint, said "He isn't the heroic figure everyone thinks he is. He is just flesh and blood, and flesh and blood can be killed."

The father, sipping on some brandy turned to Brent and said, "You need this woman son. She is your last chance. You fucked-up every other relationship you had. You are a fucking loser, but this woman is too blind to see it."

Brent, used to his father's derisive tone, said, "OK, I'm a fuck-up, but this broad adores me pop. She is mesmerized by me. I got this broad under my thumb. She is mine except for one thing. That asshole Adams keeps trying to tell her I am no good for her. It's a real chore for me to always be on my toes to counter his moves. That bitch transsexual girl was about to cause trouble, but I took care of that freak easily."

Brent's father shook his head vigorously and screamed, "Stupid bastard. You shouldn't have killed that freak of nature. That is a lose end that might come back to haunt you." He shook his head again, continuing. "What's done is done. Right now, there is a chance for you to hook up with a beautiful dame who can earn good money too. This is a win-win situation for you boy. We got to stick together as a family, just like always and take this dude out before he wises the bitch up."

"Brent's brother Harold, still puffing away, said So, what we gonna do pop? How we taking this dude out?"

First, Brent you tail Adams. I want to know all his habits. We are gonna hit him when he least expects it. He may be old, but he is sharp. The man's been through some tough situations. We gotta be careful with this one. We done things like this before, but we ain't never iced a dude as smart as Adams, or as ruthless. Mess up, and he'll come after us. That I don't want, cause I heard too many tales about what happened to others who pissed him off. This dude is tough."

Brent smiled at his pop and said, "Yeah, but not as tough and ruthless as us."

Laughing, Harold and Pop McCord shouted together, "Damn right!"

Aaron was sitting in his office when the phone rang. "Hello, Adam's Investigations."

It was like a Brahms' lullaby as the soft, melodic voice seemed to float on the air, "Hi there Aaron. How are you doing?"

"I am doing great now Jasmine, just great. It is so wonderful to hear your voice, so wonderful darling."

"Nice to hear yours too Aaron. I have missed talking to you." You could hear the sincerity in her voice thought Aaron. She really did miss talking to him.

"So, how is the job going?"

You could sense the trepidation in her voice as she said, "Great Aaron, just great, but I think about Denise all the time. I just can't believe that she would fall off the cliff like that."

Aaron said, "She didn't fall. She was pushed or thrown. I'll prove it if you want. You have two bedrooms there. Why not let me stay a couple of days and check things out?"

Very hesitantly, she said "Well, as long as you know that I will not sleep with you. Those days are over. Also, what will you do if Brent comes up?"

"I don't expect to sleep with you, and when Brent comes up I will be civil. However, I can assure you he won't be. Civility is not part of his makeup."

Sighing, Jasmine said "Don't criticise the man I love Aaron. You are right, he is uncouth and rude. I know that, but I still love him. You are going to have to get used to that fact."

"I'll accept it, but I'll never get used to it. You deserve better."

"OK, I don't want to argue, but I would like to see you. When are you coming up?"

Aaron, without hesitation said, "On my way in an hour. See you in three."

"OK, sounds good. See you then."

Time with Jasmine was golden to Aaron, and they sat up most of the night just talking. It was difficult for him to go to a separate bedroom, but he did it without complaint or pleading. He was with her again, sharing time, revelling in that beautiful smile, basking in the gloriousness of her soft melodic voice that was like a vapour on the soft summer air and soaking up the penetrating shine of those sparkling dark eyes that danced like stars in the midnight sky.

The next morning, over breakfast, they discussed Denise. Aaron was the first to broach the subject. "Denise didn't particularly like Brent did she?"

"Aaron don't go there. Brent may be a bit rough around the edges, lack manners, even be a bit prone to violence in certain situations, but he did not kill Denise. He had no reason to kill her."

Aaron wanted to be careful with what he said, as he wanted to avoid angering her. However, it was difficult. "OK. I am trying to be as diplomatic as possible, but people like him are prone to be very provincial in their outlook and un-accepting of alternative lifestyles. They are the people who have no religion, but are still influenced by it. These are the idiots who say, "Too bad your kids were slaughtered by a deranged man with an AK-47, but my right to bear arms trumps their rights to live. These are the people who want to electrocute murderers, but proclaim the sanctity of the Bible that says *thou shall not kill*. You have told me how he makes fun of homosexuals. Well, he is probably too dumb to know that Denise and trandgendered girls like her are not homosexuals. They are simply women trapped in a man's body. You really think this man believes she is a woman? Come on. He would find her offensive."

"OK, maybe he would, but that doesn't mean he would kill her."

"Darling, please let me explain something to you about men like Brent. They live their lives in quiet desperation. Things they don't understand they attack. There are no shades of grey in their lives, only black and white. There is no room for compromise. Everything is either – or. When confronted with anomalies of nature like Denise, their reaction is always negative."

Jasmine got up, walked over to the kitchen counter and poured another cup of coffee. "OK, granted he is uncompromising, stubborn and provincial in his thinking. I agree, but that doesn't make him a killer."

"No, it doesn't, but you have to have an open mind if we are going to pursue this. You see, he would consider Denise an aberration. Yet, his uncleanliness, his drug taking, his disregard for proper decorum in social situations are aberrations of another type. He could never see that, because in his world, there is only what is right and wrong, and nothing in between."

Jasmine sighed and said "Agreed Aaron, OK? He is uncouth, unmannered, as unsophisticated a man as I have ever seen. I admit it, and I don't know why I love him but I do!"

Aaron smiled at her and said, "You don't love him. You love what is between his legs."

Jasmine, smiling, replied, "Yeah, it is a nice one alright, and he knows how to use it."

It wasn't really funny thought Aaron, but I will laugh anyway, because I want to stay on her good side. I want to try and understand that she is infatuated with this man for some mysterious reasons that I simply can't comprehend.

They strolled together out to the cliff. Both of them stood there, staring down at the rocks about 50 feet below, as they listened to the waves from the lake gently lap at the rocks. How ironic thought Aaron that death could come calling for such a nice person at this beautiful spot.

Denise had always been forced to live life on the outside looking in, because she suffered from gender dysphasia. Her name had originally been Don, but living in a progressive state like New York made it possible for her to not only change her name, but also change her birth certificate from male to female with the affirmation from a psychiatrist that she suffered from gender dysphoria. Ah, thought Aaron – how lucky she was to be born in New York rather than some place like Mississippi. Unfortunately, even in New York there were backward finger-pointing bigots of stupidity who wanted to stay in the Dark Ages. Brent was one of those men who couldn't accept diversity when it came to sexuality. Nor, despite the lack of religious conviction, could he accept that someone could suffer from gender dysphoria. You were either a man or a woman or gay or straight. And if you were gay, in his mind, you were an abomination. Aaron simply could not fathom how someone as open-minded and accepting as Jasmine could embrace a man who looked with disdain on those he deemed "perverts." This simply was not the woman that he loved so much.

As they stood there silently staring at the lake, Aaron said "So, what was her reason for calling me do you think?"

Hanging her head, Jasmine said, "She wanted to tell you I was cheating on you. That is it pure and simple. She was appalled and I knew it. Yet, she said nothing derogatory to me."

Aaron walked around the cliff edge, looking for the minutest clue that might have been overlooked by the police as he said, "Denise was a good woman who had all the odds stacked against her. You don't believe she fell do you?"

"I don't know Aaron. I know that you want it to be Brent who killed her though. You hate him, because I love him."

Aaron shook his head. "No, I hate him because he is not worthy of you. I hate him because he has bewitched you with a manipulative facade that makes you swoon over him. I can see through the man to his core. His core is corrupt and has no solid foundation. He is filled with enmity and hostility toward that which he does not understand. He is blinded by his prejudices that keep him imprisoned in a way of life that is from the Dark Ages."

Deep down, Jasmine knew Aaron was right, but she was thinking with her heart, not her mind, or maybe she was just thinking with her hormones which raged with excitement when she got around Brent. Yes, that was it. Her hormones were ruling her thought processes.

Aaron bent down and noticed a slight scuff on a rock. It had been dry for weeks so it had not been washed away. The scuff was obviously made from a white tennis shoe. A small, almost microscopic piece of vinyl was imbedded in the side of the rock. Aaron looked at Jasmine as he pointed down at the scuff mark. "She was murdered. The killer stood here and tossed her body over the cliff. There is the scuff mark from his shoe."

Jasmine sighed and said, "So your next question is did Brent have white tennis shoes as the scuff is obviously from white vinyl."

Aaron just stood and waited and then when silence ensued, he said, "I'm waiting. Does he have tennis shoes with white vinyl on the heels and sides? Does he?"

Jasmine, stoically replied "Yes, Aaron. Yes he does. Happy now?"

Aaron shaking his head, replied, "No, I am not happy, because Denise is still dead."

Aaron laid his handkerchief over the scuff mark and said, "We have to call the sheriff."

Yes, I suppose so, and I also suppose Brent will be the primary suspect."

"Who else? That scuff mark is the link to the killer and he has white vinyl sneakers."

As Aaron and Jasmine strolled back toward the house, they did not notice the solitary figure crouching behind a huge rock on the nearby hillside. Brent, had observed them, and he immediately knew what was up. Aaron had found something on the rock and covered it with his handkerchief.

Brent very adroitly moved to the cliff, lifted the handkerchief and began to rub the vinyl scuff off with his own handkerchief. He rubbed furiously until there was nothing left. He was seething with anger, knowing that Jasmine was with Aaron, but he could not afford to show his face. He very quietly made his way off the cliff, down to the cove where he had parked and drove back toward New York City more determined than ever to eliminate Aaron Adams so that he would have free reign with Jasmine. He had to prevent him from exercising undue influence on her. He was fouling everything up. Brent almost had her under control, but as long as Aaron kept popping in and out of her life, he would be stymied in exerting complete control, because he knew that *when the night has come and the land is covered in darkness, when the moon is the only light there is, Aaron Adams' desire for retributive justice glowed with an intensity that would burn hotter than the fires of hell.*

CHAPTER 7
THE DEATH DEALER

When strangers come calling,
We kick the newspaper under the sofa.
We tidy-up as quickly as possible,
Because we do not want anyone
To see who we really are.
That is why every morning
The mirror is our enemy,
Because we can see inside ourselves.

When the sheriff arrived there was great anticipation on the part of Aaron and Jasmine, but their enthusiasm was dulled when the handkerchief was lifted and the scuff marks were gone. "They were there, Sheriff," said Jasmine with an air of authority.

The sheriff, quizzically, replied "I don't doubt it, but obviously they are not there now."

Aaron, a look of determination on his face, said "Will you reopen the case on our word that the scuffs were there?"

"I will Mr. Adams. I will, but the evidence is awfully flimsy. There is nothing really tangible upon which we can even embark on an investigation. We talked to Jasmine and to Brent McCord. They were the only ones present."

Aaron, a man known and respected by the sheriff, almost pleaded "I know, and I think you suspect that Brent McCord is the killer."

"Suspecting and proving are two different things. There is absolutely nothing connecting McCord with Denise. He just happened to be here while she was present. That is coincidence, nothing more, unless Jasmine here could confirm that there was animosity between them."

Jasmine, shaking her head from side to side emphatically said, "Brent McCord isn't capable of murder. He is a gentle man who just happens to be a little rough around the edges."

The sheriff looked at Aaron, then back at Jasmine, then back at Aaron again. "You two seem to have divergent opinions on Mr. McCord."

Aaron, now getting perturbed, said "We do. You see, Jasmine is in love with him, so his flaws are not apparent to her I am afraid."

"I know the two of them are having an affair Mr. Adams. I am a rural sheriff, but I am not an idiot. I checked her, him and even you out in regards to your whereabouts. It seems only you have a solid alibi Mr. Adams. Jasmine, your alibi is simply that you were her friend, but friends have arguments that can lead to murder."

Aaron, shocked at the Sheriff's suggestion that Jasmine might be implicated, shouted, "Hey, you are way off base there sheriff."

"I know she didn't do it. I am just making a point. You and I both know where the finger should be pointing, but without a direct link, without a shred of evidence, I cannot move forward against Mr. McCord. You know that."

Aaron, somewhat contritely, replied "Sorry sheriff. Yes, I know you are stymied. However, I do not work under the same restraints you do. I'm going after McCord. I am going to prove he killed her."

Jasmine turned and stormed down the hillside toward the house, obviously perturbed by Aaron's accusations against Brent. The sheriff made a waving motion with his hand, said "good luck" and proceeded up the hillside toward his car. He glanced back over his shoulder at Aaron and said, "That woman's infatuated. I met that asshole. Can't figure out what see sees in him."

Aaron nodded his head in agreement and headed back toward the house. A livid Jasmine was waiting at the kitchen table. "I'm sick of you degrading Brent. I love him. Just because of that you hate him. You can't stand him because he has me. He has what you want."

Aaron, being careful not to raise his voice, said "I want to tell you a story Jasmine as best as I can. It was often told by Socrates but originated with Plato" He eased into a chair across from here, sighed and began his tale.

"Ask yourself how much our nature is enlightened or unenlightened. Imagine human beings living in an underground den, which has a mouth open towards the light and reaching all along the den; here they have been from their childhood, and have their legs and necks chained so that they cannot move, and can only see before them, being prevented by the chains from turning round their heads. Above and behind them a fire is blazing at a distance, and between the fire and the prisoners there is a raised way; and you will see, if you look, a low wall built along the way, like the screen which marionette players have in front of them, over which they show the puppets. Men were passing along the wall carrying all sorts of vessels, and statues and figures of animals made of wood and stone and various materials, which appear over the wall? Some of them are talking, others silent. "

Jasmine interrupted. "Is there a point to this tale?

"Be patient darling. These people see only their own shadows, or the shadows of one another, which the fire throws on the opposite side wall."

Aaron shifted his position and continued in earnest. "And of the objects which are being carried in like manner they would only see the shadows? And as they conversed with one another, they were naming what was actually before them? Now, consider further that this prison had an echo which came from the other side, and they assumed when one of the passers-by spoke that the voice which they heard came from the passing shadow. To them, the truth would be literally nothing but the shadows of the images. Now, ask yourself what would naturally follow if the prisoners were released and disabused of their error. At first, when any of them is liberated and compelled suddenly to stand up and turn his neck round and walk and look towards the light, he will suffer sharp pains; the glare will distress him, and he will be unable to see the realities of which in his former state he had seen the shadows; and then conceive some one saying to him, that what he saw before was an illusion, but that now, when he is approaching nearer to being and his eye is turned towards more real existence, he has a clearer vision, what will be his reply? And you may further imagine that his instructor is pointing to the objects as they pass and requiring him to name them. Will he not be perplexed? Will he not fancy that the shadows which he formerly saw are truer than the objects which are now shown to him? And if he is compelled to look straight at the light, will he not have a pain in his eyes which will make him turn away to take in the objects of vision which he can see, and which he will conceive to be in reality clearer than the things which are now being shown to him? And suppose once more, that he is reluctantly dragged up a steep and rugged ascent, and held fast until he's forced into the presence of the sun itself, is he not likely to be pained and irritated? When he approaches the light his eyes will be dazzled, and he will not be able to see anything at all of what are now called realities. He will require growing accustomed to the sight of the upper world. And first he will see the shadows best, next the reflections of men and other objects in the water, and then the objects themselves; then he will gaze upon the light of the moon and the stars and the heavens; and he will see the sky and the stars by night better than the sun or the light of the sun by day? Last of all, he will be able to see the sun, and not mere reflections of him in the water, but he will see him in his own proper place, and not in another; and he will contemplate him as he is. He will then proceed to argue that this is he who gives the season and the years, and is the guardian of all that is in the visible world, and in a certain way the cause of all things which he and his fellows have been accustomed to behold? And when he remembered his old habitation, and the wisdom of the den and his fellow-prisoners, do you not suppose that he would felicitate himself on the change, and pity them?"

Jasmine, beginning to understand the parable, said "Certainly, he would."

Aaron continued: "And if they were in the habit of conferring honours among themselves on those who were quickest to observe the passing shadows and to remark which of them went before, and which followed after, and which were together; and who were therefore best able to draw conclusions as to the future, do you think that he would care for such honours and glories, or envy the possessors of them? Would he not say with it is better to live in the light than the darkness."

Aaron paused for awhile and said "So, what do you think?"

"Yes, I think that he would rather suffer anything than entertain these false notions and live in that miserable manner."

Aaron felt that he was beginning to reach her. "Imagine once more, suddenly out of the sun to be replaced in his old situation; would he not be certain to have his eyes full of darkness? And if there were a contest, and he had to compete in measuring the shadows with the prisoners who had never moved out of the den, while his sight was still weak, and before his eyes had become steady (and the time which would be needed to acquire this new habit of sight might be very considerable) would he not be ridiculous? Men would say of him that up he went and down he came without his eyes; and that it was better not even to think of ascending."

Bowing her head and thinking, Jasmine suddenly blurted out "And what is the purpose of this allegorical decent into ridiculousness?"

Aaron smiled and said "That you may now see that the prison-house is the world of sight, the light of the fire is the sun, and you will not misapprehend me if you interpret the journey upwards to be the ascent of the soul into the intellectual world, which, at your desire, I have expressed whether rightly or wrongly as a world of reality as opposed to a world of shadows. In the world of knowledge the idea of good appears last of all, and is seen only with an effort; and, when seen, is also inferred to be the universal author of all things beautiful and right, parent of light and of the lord of light in this visible world, and the immediate source of reason and truth in the intellectual; and that this is the power upon which he who would act rationally, either in public or private life must have his or her eyes fixed. In other words, you darling have fallen victim to the shadows of a man who has not revealed his real self to you. He hides his real self in the shadows and you see what he projects as the truth, but it is an illusion created by a master magician."

She said not a word. She just sat and thought about what Aaron was saying. Had she been fooled? Did she only see shadows on the wall and not the real Brent?

"OK Aaron, I agree that the man may not, beneath the surface, be what I think he is. I know that he harbours deep psychological scars. I know that he is, indeed, capable of perpetrating cruelties upon those whom he considers outside societal norms. He has no religion, but is still affected by its most base prejudices. I know he is uncouth and has horrible manners when it comes to the common niceties. I never said he was a very intelligent man or that he possessed the common social graces of polite society. I know all this, but I still love him. What am I to do?"

Aaron, very sympathetically said "You are lucky, as I am like Jesus today. I have a parable for every situation. Let me tell you another story."

"In ancient times, a King had a boulder placed on a roadway. Then he hid himself and watched to see if anyone would remove the huge rock. Some of the kingdom's wealthiest merchants and courtiers came by and simply walked around it. Many loudly blamed the king for not keeping the roads clear, but none did anything about getting the stone out of the way. Then a peasant came along carrying a load of vegetables. Upon approaching the boulder, the peasant laid down his burden and tried to move the stone to the side of the road. After much pushing and straining, he finally succeeded. After the peasant picked up his load of vegetables, he noticed a purse lying in the road where the boulder had been. The purse contained many gold coins and a note from the king indicating that the gold was for the person who removed the boulder from the roadway. The peasant learned what many of us never understand. Every obstacle presents an opportunity to improve our condition." Aaron smiled and continued, "My dear Jasmine. You have a chance to learn, grow and improve your condition."

She looked at Aaron and said "I love you Aaron Adams!"

Aaron did not doubt it. She did love him, but she also still loved Brent. Aaron had to prove to her that Brent was not the man she thought he was. Aaron thought of something he had once read:

A man found a cocoon of a butterfly.
One day a small opening appeared.
He sat and watched the butterfly for several hours
as it struggled to squeeze through the tiny hole.
Then it stopped, as if it couldn't go further.
So the man decided to help the butterfly.
He took a pair of scissors and

snipped off the remaining bits of cocoon.
The butterfly emerged easily but
it had a swollen body and shrivelled wings.

The man continued to watch it,
expecting that any minute the wings would enlarge
and expand enough to support the body,
Neither happened!
In fact the butterfly spent the rest of its life
crawling around.
It was never able to fly.

What the man in his kindness
and haste did not understand:
The restricting cocoon and the struggle
required to get through the opening
was a way of forcing the fluid from the body
into the wings so that it would be ready
for flight once that was achieved.

Sometimes struggles are exactly
what we need in our lives.
Going through life with no obstacles would
cripple and enfeeble us.
We will not be as strong as we could have been
and we would never fly.

Aaron was not going to completely open the cocoon for Jasmine. He was going to let things happen naturally, so she would see the real Brent and be able to fly free of his influence.

J. Wayne Frye   121

As was his custom, Brent sent smiley faces and messages throughout the day to Jasmine and expected her to always be available in the evenings for his calls. Any divergence from the norm by her raised a red flag of suspicion in his mind, as he knew that she was a very desirable woman, and that he had to be eternally vigilant against anyone else stealing what he now felt was his property. He had invested time, and most of all, money that he did not have in wooing her. As he paid off the loans he incurred through frivolous spending to pursue her, he kept thinking that it was a wise investment, because he had a prize that all her men wanted and now they would look at him with envy, because he had won her. His ego gratification was the driving force that made him beg, borrow and steal to woo her, and he had even committed murder to make sure she was his, and he was preparing to commit murder for the second time to ensure his total victory. This was a war between him and Aaron Adams. His ego could not take the loss of this remarkable woman who had foolishly fallen for a man who was all façade and no core. His was a lonely existence in pursuit of that which made him feel worthwhile, feel like he was of value in a world that had always looked with disdain on him. He was more boy than man, but the boy in him longed for recognition, and with Jasmine by his side, he got that recognition from family, friends and co-workers who marvelled that he could win such an extraordinary woman. He was flying high and would do whatever it took to make sure he kept the woman who massaged his ego and made it possible for him to proudly prove his worth by having her by his side. It was not love of Jasmine, but love of self that drove him. With her, he was somebody. He had worth as a human being because, with her by his side, he was envied by one and all.

Brent's father ran a corner deli off Northern Boulevard in the Woodside section of Queens, made famous as the home to Archie Bunker. Ironically, Brent's father's deli was only a short distance from 704 Houser Street, which was the residence of the fictional Archie. How appropriate thought Aaron as he heard Mr. McCord say something to white patron as he handed him his order over the counter. What he said would be music to Archie's bigoted ears. "Yeah, them niggers and spicks is always causing trouble out here. This place used to be a white neighbourhood and one of these days we real Americans will take our guns and make it white again."

Aaron eased forward as the man took his package and left. McCord, through dingy teeth said "Yes sir. What can I do you for?"

Aaron, always disdainful of those who thought that whites were the favoured race, said "Don't know, when's the KKK meeting tonight?"

McCord, every bit as arrogant as his son, replied, "Fuck you asshole. I don't need your business. Take a hike."

Aaron leaned in real close and said, "Well, maybe the Human Rights Commissioner would like to hear about your attitude. Someone should inform you that discrimination is illegal in New York City."

You could see the pulsating veins beginning to stick out in McOrd's neck. "Yeah, well tell the Human Rights Commissioner to shove it up its ass, too!"

Aaron was smiling now as he saw McCord reach under the counter, obviously for a gun. Aaron put his hand inside his left breast pocket and said "Don't pull it McCord. Mine's bigger and more deadly. The name's Aaron Adams."

McCord very slowly brought his hand back out from under the counter, obviously empty. "What you want Adams? Your business would be with my son, not me."

"True, but I hear you are a close family, so I just want to get to know all of you. Your son's an asshole, and you can tell him I said so. From my observation, he must come by it naturally. My guess is that your other son is an asshole, too. My inclination, frankly, is that you are a family of real assholes."

All the time, Aaron was incessantly smiling that deadly smile that hit an adversary right in the pit of the stomach and let him know Aaron was not afraid of him. McCord was not physically trembling, but Aaron knew he was on the inside. McCord was a man who loved to intimidate others, and even in his 60's, he was obviously still a formable man, but you could see in his psyche that Aaron had him scared, had him guessing just how far Aaron would go. This gave Aaron the edge.

"So, my guess is that your son, and I am sure you, think transgender people are sick individuals."

Even fear did not make the arrogance subside. "They are perverted fucks that should use their dicks for what God intended them to use them for – fucking women. A man going around in makeup, wigs, dresses and dainty little panties is an abomination, and that comes right from the Bible."

"Oh, so you are an expert on the Bible? Maybe I should call you the Reverend McCord. Last time I checked, Jesus hung out with 12 men. Maybe he was a little on the gay side himself. Doesn't seem too kosher for a straight guy to hang out with 12 men."

"Listen you blasphemous asshole, state your business and get out."

"My business is that I am going to bring your son down for the murder of Denise Coleman. I think you know he did it. I'm coming for him, and if you or your other son gets in my way, you're going down, too."

He was growing angrier now. "Adams, you are fucking with the wrong people. We aren't intimidated by assholes like you."

"Intimidated or not, you know I am not the kind of man you want to mess with. Your son has fooled Jasmine, but I am older and wiser than she is. I see through his little game of ego gratification. My guess is that Brent having her also elevates your ego, because you never figured your son capable of landing a woman of quality like Jasmine. Guess what? She will eventually come to her senses, and when she does, she will give Brent his walking papers."

Aaron noticed McCord's right hand edging under the counter again. "Go for it asshole. Go ahead." Aaron stared at McCord without blinking as he continued. "I have a big bastard of a 45 that is just itching to spit some lead. Go ahead, as Clint Eastwood used to say, "Make my day."

Again McCord backed off, and Aaron snickered at him. "Guys like you need your guns and religion, because you think that is what being an American is all about. You think that gun makes you a man. It's an extension of your dick, because you probably can't get your dick up anymore, but you can always whip out that gun, get it up, and have it ejaculate hot lead that gives you that euphoric feeling you used to get when you pumped sperm into a woman."

Aaron was having fun goading McCord. He knew he was too smart to pull the gun, but he enjoyed bringing down the arrogant who somehow thought they were tough. Hell, McCord didn't know what tough was when compared to a man like Aaron. So, Aaron let him have a tirade of vindictiveness that could only come from someone who really knew what tough was. "Talk to some of your Hispanic neighbours once in awhile and ask them what Caballerismo means. A real tough guy's manliness is based on honour and chivalry. You have neither. Real machismo is about honour, responsibility, perseverance and courage. Real men understand masculinity is not about dominating and controlling a woman, but about nurturing her and respecting her autonomy, and never using violence against her."

McCord was seething with anger and hatred, which made Aaron joyfully continue. "Projecting toughness that's unproven is one of the gravest sins of character a man can commit. McCord, men like you and your sons think that women are property and that you own them. Let me tell you something, nobody is going to own Jasmine Alexander Adams as long as I am alive."

McCord just stood there taking Aaron's derisive comments, because he knew that Aaron was the kind of man you killed from behind, not to his face. Aaron Adams was a dangerous man.

Aaron was really enjoying himself now. "Toughness is a nebulous concept at best. Fundamentally, people like you associate it with someone's ability to exercise physical violence. Someone who's good at kicking lots of ass is tough, according to you and people like you? Well, maybe. On the other hand, someone who bullies the weak is actually weak himself and cruel, so physical toughness has no absolute measure. And let me tell you something, a gun does not make you tough. In fact, it makes you weak. If you have to have a gun to prove your manliness, then you are no man at all. You 2nd Amendment loving freaks need a gun, because you think that makes you a man. It actually makes you a wimp. A man who needs a gun is weak and ineffectual. I carry a gun because I have to deal so often with assholes like you who are packing. That gun under your counter isn't to protect your business. It is to protect your masculinity. Without that gun, you are not a man."

"I have dealt with men like you all my life – flag waving, Jesus loving, gun toting assholes who think patriotism is standing up for your country right or wrong. People like you are the problem with this nation. You are anachronisms that flourish in a nation that lets fools like you brandish your guns and shout halleluiah in the public square. You and your sons think that might makes right. Well, you are now dealing with a man who can go toe-to-toe with you on your own level, so watch out McCord. You have never dealt with a man like me before. Believe me, what I am capable of you couldn't even imagine. Cruelty was taught to me by the master – the U.S. Army."

Then Aaron turned his back, as he prepared to walk out of the deli and said, "OK, here's my back, asshole. Go ahead, pull that gun out, but think long and hard before you do it, because my instincts were honed in war. The slightest movement, the slightest alteration in your breathing, and I will have my hand inside my coat as I turn around and the death dealer will be out like a flash of lightning spitting lead into your face before you even have that gun raised and your finger on the trigger."

Aaron walked out of the deli with his back to McCord as McCord stood perfectly still fearful that the slightest move might be a miscalculation that would make Aaron reach for the death dealer.

CHAPTER 8
RESPITE FROM THE STORMS OF DISMAY

Fierce hunger reigns within his breast.
He had suffered the cruellest of blows.
His spirit was crushed by she whom he loved.
Bitter was his essence of unrest.
Sorrow had been hurled upon his heart.

Each ebbing breath was but a cry
That bespoke of the agony within.
His mind knelled with agony and one thought.
What if he would spend his life
Nevermore to touch her softness?

Through the void of night he searched.
How he ached for she who had his heart.
She sat upon a throne looking down,
As he knelt begging for a sign of hope.
Ah, but when he glanced up, he was alone.

He hungered for her forlornly.
Perchance a comfort awaited him
To penetrate his aching heart.
From the solemn deep far voices cry out
Questioning why they are apart.

Wherever he goes, even in a crowd
He is alone, isolated from the world,
As within his heart is a raging pain
That knows absolutely no end.

The Girl Who Motivated Murder Most Foul

There is a blank where life once was.

Be thy heart stilled with false hope?
Can not the winds of optimism
Blow sweetly among the trees
That dot a forest within a land
Where love and tranquility abide?

Aaron felt good. He had struck first blood. Yes, the father would relate to Brent what was coming, and Brent would, with anticipatory relish, look forward to battling Aaron for the hand of she who was so fair. But Aaron was not battling him hand-to-hand. He was battling him intellectually, trying to expose the evil for Jasmine to see, so that she would finally be able to comprehend the depths of depravity in a man who was all façade. Once you opened the door, you would see the false front that hid the corruption of soul that was inside.

How do you prove a man guilty of murder when the only clue has been eradicated? Confession may be good for the soul, but Brent had no soul. All he had was an ego that needed the gratification supplied by one Jasmine Alexander. She was what gave his life meaning now, and he was not about to give that up without fight. Brent McCord was a desperate man. So desperate that he would resort to any means to keep that which massaged his ego and gratified his deep rooted need to have people respect him. Jasmine gave him that respect.

There are many different levels of criminal psychology. In this case, Aaron knew that killing was not a crime in Brent's mind, because he had killed what he considered an abomination. Justification was easy. Denise was not really a person. She was just a freak of nature who had no place in society. Oddly, in Brent's case, Aaron deduced that the killing was material as well as psychological, because there was a prize connected. Jasmine was the thing of material value, and Brent needed to protect his investment. His time, his lying, his manipulation and his money were all tied up in her. He could let nothing stand in the way of his need to gratify his ego.

Brent had honed his skill as a manipulator and liar through years of practice. No doubt, he had acted impulsively when he killed Denise, but he was also methodical in the way he covered it up. He was not a smart man intellectually, but he was smart when it came to subterfuge, manipulation and concealing the truth. He had total disregard for the laws when it came to people like Denise, as she was, in his mind, not even a person.

Brent was driven by strong feelings of anger and resentment, flowing from beliefs about being persecuted or grossly mistreated. He viewed himself as carrying out a highly personal agenda of payback when attacking someone.

To the very last I grapple with thee.
From hell's heart I stab at thee.
For hate's sake I spit my last breath at thee.
Thus, I give up the spear of my tortured soul
To imbed deep within your heart.
Hate! Hate! Hate! That is my cry to thee.

Aaron had known men like Brent all his life. They were tortured souls who floundered in uselessness until they found that one spark of hope that watered their egos and made them flower with hope. Jasmine was Brent's last hope, his last chance to prove his worth to the world. He could not let that go! And his soul was tortured with hate for Aaron, because he knew that Aaron could see through him deep within his soul. He had managed to adroitly keep his shallowness hidden from Jasmine, but Aaron was more astute at seeing beneath the surface. It had been the nature of his business for so many years that he could read people like no one else could. He was more than just a detective; he was a psychological prober of the minds of men and women who could reach through to the depths of their souls and scrape off the varnish that hid the real person.

Aaron paid a visit to his old friend John Havoc at the 87th Precinct and after the customary niceties, Aaron said, "So, I know McCord killed her John, but where do I find a thread, something, anything that might point the finger at him?"

"Aaron, it's understandable, because of the situation, but you are too close to the case. You can't see things because you are too wrapped up in hate – hate for a man who stole your life from you. You have to back off and be more objective. See things unclouded by this intense hatred."

Aaron nodded his head in agreement. "You are right John, but it is difficult. I have gone after worse men in my career, but I have never gone after anyone I hated this much."

"OK, let's take a drive to Finger Lakes tomorrow. We'll go back over the case step by step."

"You're on John, and thanks. I appreciate it."

"No problem Aaron. I owe you big time and you know it. I would like to see Jasmine anyway."

John was not the kind of man to interject himself into friends' business, and he avoided mentioning the breakup. He, Aaron and Jasmine had a pleasant lunch and than wandered out to the cliff afterward.

"So, Jasmine," said John, "describe to me exactly what you saw. Start with your walk up here from the house and tell me everything from the time you walked out the kitchen door."

Jasmine reflected back on that day and began: "I stood by the screen door and told Brent that I was going to look for Denise. He said 'OK, be careful on the path as it is treacherous.' So, I told him I would be and headed up the narrow pathway."

Aaron interrupted. "But you didn't say that when the sheriff was interviewing you. You just said you left and went up the pathway. How did Brent know it was treacherous? Had he ever been up here before?"

Jasmine was in deep thought for a few seconds and said "No, he had never been up there as far as I know, but he must have known it was a bit difficult as you could see from the cabin that it was a long and winding path. He obviously just assumed it."

Aaron and John looked at one another with a quizzical countenance. Had he planted that seed in Jasmine's mind intentionally to justify Denise's fall?

John said, "Continue."

"Well, I went up the path slowly, not getting too close to the edge as I got toward the top. I could hear the waves from the lake gently lapping against the rocks below, and I thought how pleasant the sound was."

Aaron said, "Did you stop along the way at all?"

"I did," and she turned and pointed back at a clearing about 20 feet away. "Right down there."

They all three walked back down to the clearing where they just stood and looked around for a few seconds. Aaron noticed a broken branch on a small bush and asked, "Was that broken like that when you came looking for her?"

"Yes, I remember that it was, as at the time the broken branch was on the ground. It is gone now."

Aaron looked at the two of them and said "Wait here. I need to get something. I'll be right back."

A few minutes later Aaron came walking up the hillside with something large thrown over his back. It was a blanket, and inside it he had placed several pillows. He stopped near the broken branch and began to put some rocks in the pillow cases. "I'd say that Denise weighed about 90 kilos (around 200 pounds)," he said as John began to help him with the rocks. They lifted it and agreed it must be 90 kilos. Aaron wrapped the rocks in the sheet, tied it off at both ends and then slung it over his shoulder. As he did so, he proceeded up the path and intentionally moved near the branch. The bundle brushed against it.

Again, Aaron and John looked at one another while Jasmine took a deep breath and sighed as she realized that someone could have carried Denise's body up the path and accidentally hit the branch with it.

Aaron continued up the path and stopped where he and Jasmine had seen the scuff marks. He wedged his foot in the same place and tossed the bundle over the side. It fell onto the rocks below, and he turned to Jasmine. "Take a look. Is that approximately where the body was resting?"

"Yes, almost exact."

Aaron was now convinced beyond any doubt that Denise was murdered. He understood Newton's laws of physics in enough detail to know that the body was tossed over simply by the way it landed on the rocks. Had she fallen, and been conscious, she would have fought violently on the way down, altering the trajectory and would have fallen further from the shore, as she would have no doubt, struggled to fling her body further out to hit the water rather than the rocks.

Aaron reached in his coat pocket and removed the little spiral notepad that he always carried. He sat down on a rock and began to draw. As he did so, Jasmine was in deep thought as she realized where all this was leading.

Aaron produced a drawing:

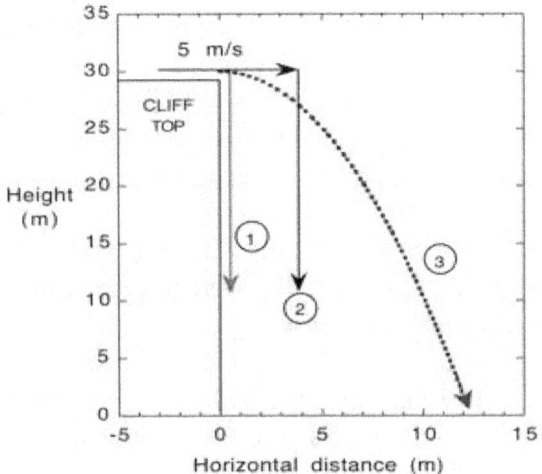

2 and 3 are the likely trajectory if she fell because she would have struggled to reach the water to survive the fall. 1 is where she actually fell, which means she was heavy and the killer couldn't toss the heavy body any further out because of the weight.

Jasmine looked at Aaron. "OK. You are right. There is no doubt that she was murdered. It still doesn't prove Brent did it."

Aaron very pensively said, "No, it only proves she was murdered, but let's look at the suspects. Who was present? You and Brent were the only two here. It isn't likely some stranger came along and just arbitrarily killed her.

Jasmine sighed. "OK, go to the sheriff with your little diagram. Go ahead. You are determined to railroad him. Go ahead." She turned and headed down the hillside, looked over her shoulder and continued, "I still don't believe it. I don't."

John looked at Aaron and said, "We need to see the sheriff and go over what we came up with. He will surely reopen the case."

"He will John, but we still need something putting Brent and Denise on the cliff together. We need a reason for him killing her."

"The reason is obvious Aaron. He simply is a cretin. He couldn't tolerate Jasmine being friends with someone he thought was a freak, and you said it yourself. She called you right before her death and left a message on your answering machine. Obviously, he probably overheard the call and took umbrage to the fact she was informing on Jasmine's extra-marital affair. For some reason, he wasn't prepared to let you know about it yet. Watch yourself Aaron. This guy is dynamite and he may explode any minute. Also, watch Jasmine, try to prevent her from being alone with him. Guys like this are dangerous. They get a woman they never dreamed of having and they will do anything to keep her."

Aaron, as he said goodbye to John thought his hardships never would come to an end! Taking long, furious strides back toward the cabin, with the collar of his coat hunched savagely up round his ears and his hands thrust in my pant's pockets, he strode along, cursing his unlucky stars the whole way. Not one real untroubled hour in so long he thought. Yet, through it all he had continued to be honourable to the heart's core. He could not bring himself to go in and talk to Jasmine. He walked in circles until deciding to get in his car and leave.

He got back to the city around 9 and parked the car in the underground garage, but strolled out to the street rather than going up to the lonely co-op. People roamed about in all directions, quiet pairs and noisy groups mixed with one another. The great hour had commenced, the pairing time when the mystic traffic is in full swing--and the hour of merry adventures sets in. Rustling feet scurrying along, sensual laughter, silly giggles, heaving bosoms, passionate, panting breaths, and far down near the Empire Hotel, a voice was shouting "Repent!" The whole street was a swamp of muck and mire, from which hot vapours of hopelessness were exuded.

He felt involuntarily in his pockets for a few lose dollar bills that he always kept neatly folded. The passion that thrills through the movements of every one of the passers-by, the dim light of the street lamps, the quiet darkness of the night, all commenced to affect him. The air that was laden with whispers, embraces, trembling admissions, concessions, half-uttered words and suppressed cries all seemed to be burdening his already weary soul. A number of cats were declaring their love with loud courting meows. His was a misery, wretchedness without parallel in his life. What humiliation, too; what disgrace to be unceremoniously tossed aside for such a low-life!

In order to console himself, to mildly indemnify himself in some measure, he took to finding possible faults in the people who glided by. He shrugged his shoulders contemptuously, and looked harshly at the people as they passed. These contemptuous people he thought actually think they are living. These young teachers, retail associates, bank clerks, merchants, financiers all fall for the marketing that tells them that happiness is only one more purchase away. These are the suckers who keep the 1% in the lap of luxury, because they actually believe in the American dream which is in reality a nightmare. They will never make it, unless they are the offspring of the privileged class. The seats at the pinnacle of the economic ladder are reserved, and very few, a miniscule few from the lower rungs, ever reach the top. How easy it was to fool people in America.

He spat out over the pavement, without troubling if it hit any one. He felt enraged; filled with contempt for these people who scraped acquaintanceship with one another, and paired off right before his eyes. He was jealous of their closeness.

An attractive, but older, maybe at least 55, woman looked fixedly at him as he passed by her. For some reason, he said, "good evening."

She nodded and said "hello there."

Hum! Why was she out walking so late? Did not a woman alone represent less than stellar intentions? "So, you lonely tonight?" asked Aaron.

She stared at Aaron with astonishment, scanned his face closely, to see what he really meant by the statement. "I am alone yes, but lonely, not really."

Aaron smiled and said, "I'll walk with you. It isn't safe for a lovely woman like you to be out all alone in this neighbourhood."

For some reason, she felt no mal-intent from Aaron and allowed him to walk with her. But when we had gone a few paces Aaron came to a standstill and said "I am not very good company I am afraid. You see, my wife left me for another man."

She smiled and said, "You can come with me if you like. My husband left me for a younger woman four months ago. I know how difficult it is."

Aaron said "No." Besides, he would still feel like he was betraying Jasmine, despite the fact that she had betrayed him.

She was more determined now. "You are coming with me. Don't argue. I am Myrna."

Aaron needed someone, anyone to assuage his loneliness. "OK. I am Aaron. Why not?"

"Well, listen to me now, Myrna!" and Aaron set about explaining his situation. The woman grew more and more astonished in measure at the love he had for Jasmine as he proceeded. He rubbed his hands with delight over the happy notions he recalled with her, and soliloquized aloud, "What a joy there is in going about knowing you love someone so much." Perhaps he thought, I have given this forlorn creature a downward impulse for her whole life because now she will reflect on her own loss and lament it even more. Did it, in truth, pay to be honourable, upright, and righteous thought Aaron, for perhaps it was wrong to pour your heart out to a stranger who was also suffering from the same agonies of losing someone who was so dear?

Yet, by talking with her, Aaron's spirits were effervescing. He felt fresh and courageous enough to face anything that might turn up. She looked at him and said, "Nothing I can do is going to deter your loneliness. I know that, but please come with me to my apartment and we shall sit and talk to one another about what we have lost. Sharing your pain with someone is cathartic. It cleanses the soul."

Aaron smiled, nodded in the affirmative, and the two went off into the quiet night in silence, knowing that they both had found someone to share their misery with, someone who was meandering down the same street of lost dreams.

Aaron recalled something he had once read: *the strongest men are the most alone.* Yes, he was with a woman, but he was still alone. He thought to himself, "this woman could give me a wild night of fornication and it would not change my loneliness." Hey it was Friday night, and people were pairing off, trying to beat the loneliness. But the truth was that there was nothing out there for anyone to really change things, because there was nothing out there but stupidity - stupid people mingling with stupid people in search of that which did not exist. Bars and clubs were filled with people, but the crowds were not an answer to loneliness. They were just facades to hide from the truth that everyone was lonely and in need of real reasons to justify their existence when there was no justification. Why do people have to be so lonely? What's the point of life? Everyone was yearning, looking to others to satisfy a primal urge to be with someone, yet most people isolated themselves without realizing it. If there was a God, maybe he was actually a devil who got great pleasure from nourishing loneliness among people. Was it funny to him as he watched people desperately try to get that which was always just out of reach.

The loneliest moment in someone's life is when they are watching their whole world fall apart, and all they can do is stare blankly as the world crumbles around them. This had been Aaron's life for some time now, and nothing seemed to change it. Long ago he stopped the pursuit of pleasure that often had periled his life with she whom he loved and tainted his personal reputation and reason. He was now just a life lost in a desperate attempt to escape from torturing memories, from a sense of insupportable loneliness and a dread of some strange impending doom. Aaron was nothing more than a dead man walking. Where hope used to exist, there was a hole in the world, which he found himself constantly walking around it in the daytime, and falling in at night as he grasp the reality of his loneliness when he came home to an empty apartment. He had lost hope. He was trapped in his own private hell.

Most people were not special he thought. People just were. Yes, they just were. 99% of them were just accidents as a result of two people being horny and throwing caution to the wind. There was no grand plan, no great scheme orchestrated by a celestial being relaxing on a cloud as he looked out for the welfare of his creations. There was only one thing anyone could be certain of when born, and that was death. Fortunately, death was genuinely the end. There was no heaven in a vast boundless space, and no brilliant light which never faded. Anyway, who would want to be among a bunch of people who were walking, praying and singing all the time while plucking celestial harps as they relaxed on a cloud? And who wanted angels flying above them all the time making noise with their flapping wings?

As they sit down over a cup of coffee, Myrna said, "So, will we ever get over our loss?"

Aaron, bowing his head a bit, said "No, we won't. We both love with to great of an intensity. When you are betrayed like we were, there seems to be no way out of the pit of despair."

Myrna sighed and offered her own dire prediction. "We are destined to be alone I guess, because of that intensity and now fear that it could happen again if we took them back, I suppose. We are dammed if we do and damned if we don't."

Aaron rose and began to walk up and down the floor. With Myrna passively looking on he gazed out the window; there was ice on the sill; it was snowing outside. Down on the sidewalk a thick layer of snow covered the pavement and was gradually piling up. Aaron bustled about the room, took aimless turns to and fro and scratched his head as if trying to figure out his next move. He leaned against the kitchen counter for a while, tapped his forefinger on the Formica countertop, and then seemed to drift off into deep thought quietly and pensively.

After a short time, he pulled myself sharply together, licked his lips and said "There must be an end to this." He moved to Myrna who stood up and looked him directly in the eyes and in a very un-lady like fashioned almost shouted, "fuck me Aaron!"

Aaron swept her in his arms and they kissed passionately and frantically with tongues battling a duel of flicking, flaying delightfulness as they embraced in rapturous ecstasy enjoying something they had both long for.

Myrna's soft right hand found its way inside Aaron's pants as she had managed to unzip him. She gripped his pulsating member and began to slowly stroke it. As their lips parted, she smiled up at him while massaging his swollen stiff shaft.

Aaron was fascinated at how deftly she managed to remove her jeans, leaving her standing before him in just a t-shirt and a pair of tight, black panties. Her magnificent breasts were braless and they bounced up and down against his chest and the warmth made his body melt with delightfulness. Aaron reached down and felt the moistness of her panties as the excitement had obviously created a discharge of fluid from the anticipatory delight over what was coming.

Her eyes locked on Aaron's eyes and she dropped to her knees, eyed the head of his member, licked her lips and sucked him deep into her mouth as Aaron unbuckled his belt and let his pants drop to the floor. He could only moan as he gripped the back of her head with both hands and pulled her toward him to make sure all his pulsating rod was down her throat. There was just a slight "cluck" sound. It slid fully down her throat until her lips were tight against his groin. Her eyes rolled back in her head as she happily sighed.

Aaron held her there for a moment before he released her head. She backed off slowly and let the head of his joy stick slip between her lips. A thin strand of saliva connected the head to her hot tongue.

"Mmm, tasty," she moaned before she engulfed his rampant shaft again. She continued moaning as she bobbed up and down, taking him fully down her throat on each delightful stroke.

He let her continue for a while, fully revelling in the sensations she created, before he pulled away. He lifted her to her feet, gripped the waistband of her panties and pulled them down. What a hairy delight he thought as he realized she was a natural woman who was not ashamed of her full growth of pubic hair that covered her from thigh to thigh and went up her waist almost to her belly button.

Aaron dropped to his knees and began to kiss, lick, suck and blow on her delightful mound of desire. "Oh," she moaned as she tilted her head back and revelled in the ecstasy of the moment.

She reached back and put her hips on the kitchen table while removing her t-shirt, thrusting out her hot, pulsating, hairy mound.

Aaron ran his hands up her torso to grip her breasts. He pinched her already-hard nipples. She dropped her hands to his head and, with a groan deep from her throat, gripped his hair as her knees buckled. "God, I think I'm gonna cum!" she moaned. "Gonna make me cum already baby!"

Aaron pulled away, forestalling her orgasm, despite her attempts to hold his head in place. He let her spit-soaked mound fall from his mouth and spun her by her hips until she was facing the far wall with her ass seemingly begging for Aaron's hot rod. He grabbed both cheeks of her beautiful, round, bubble butt and spread them wide. He leaned forward and whispered, "do you have any lubricant for that tight little hole. She reached over to the nearby refrigerator and brought out the tub of margarine. Aaron coated her up and her hands slapped at the table as she thrust her voluptuous ass out to receive Aaron's coming thrust. He began to gently massage the opening, relaxing her muscles, lubing her with the margarine. He wrapped one hand around her mound of desire while he reached up and gripped a breast with the other hand. She started trying to hump backward, almost begging for Aaron's stiff member to ram her, moaning with her face now resting on the table.

She looked back over her shoulder at Aaron, her eyes glazed with arousal and a deep longing burned into her now begging, almost pleading eyes.

"Fuck it baby," she begged. "Please, just fuck it hard!"

Aaron lined himself up with her little hole and pressed forward. She moaned as the muscles of her sphincter resisted for a moment, then groaned, as the muscular ring relaxed and the head of

Aaron's stiff member popped through and into her most intimate chamber of delightfulness.

"Oh, Yes!" she longingly moaned. "Yeah, baby!"

Aaron paused for a moment, reset his feet. He pulled back slightly and drove forward. Most of his member just surged into her rectum, spreading her muscles, eliciting a deep, "Ugh," from her throat. One more push and he was buried balls-deep inside her and she was moaning like she had found nirvana.

She moaned deep as he reached around, grabbed her hairy mound and started stroking in time with his thrusts into her anal cavity. She was mumbling incoherently as he gave her the Aaron Adams special, gradually building up speed, until he was slamming deep and hard into her clenching, receptive hole that was now completely relaxed.

She was hot inside, her rectal muscles rippling, gripping and releasing his member. She started thrusting back against him as he grabbed her tit, alternating, manipulating the tiny, firm orb with pinching and pulling, twisting her erect nipples.

Aaron began to almost lift her off the floor with each thrust as she moaned "Ummm," while she began to artfully grip and then release his love muscle. She had obviously had this kind of sex often as she was incredibly adapt at working her sphincter to maximum affect, almost squeezing the joy juice from Aaron's hot throbbing member that had found a home where it felt warm and loved.

"Ooooh, yeah!" she moaned as he resumed pounding her furiously. His penetration seemed to get deeper and deeper as he filled her repeatedly with his shaft. Aaron tilted her chest sideways so he could get her breast in his mouth while still pounding. The diamond-hard nipple and most of the breast behind it fit perfectly into his mouth. Her head flew back and she literally screamed as the sensations coursed through her alluring body.

She was on the verge of exploding but Aaron didn't want her to cum, because he had other things in mind. Before she could reach her peak, he gave a few more solid thrusts into her hot hole and suddenly he whispered, "Let it happen Myrna, go ahead, let it happen. Cum baby, cum!"

The explosion was almost like a bomb blast as she let out a blood-curdling deafening roar while the intense organism rocked through her body at the same time Aaron was depositing his seed deep inside her ass with such a fury that she could feel it pounding viciously against her insides. Oh, what a glorious coupling it was. Each squirt from

Aaron's throbbing member was met with a spasm that rocked Myrna's body as she delightfully cum with an intensity she had never experienced before. They were both satiated with exhaustion, but so intense was the coupling that they could not let the delightfulness rest on just one cum.

Aaron whispered into her ear, suck it hard again and I will do it even more furiously for you. She immediately turned around and dropped to her knees, working furiously to make it rock hard again so that she could enjoy the incredible titillating joy that had rocked her so violently before. She craved it. She was a slave to desire, a prisoner of lasciviousness of the basest kind. She was overwhelmed with yearning passion and lecherous salacity. She was a woman on fire.

Aaron began to thrust his member in and out of her mouth as she sucked with a fury. She pulled away; again placed her magnificent ass in the air as she leaned forward on the kitchen table and told Aaron, "Give it to me again baby. Please!"

Aaron put the head back into place and pushed inside with ease this time as she was wide open and ready for action. Again she moaned with contented felicity as Aaron started his rhythmic pounding, building up speed steadily as she reached back to feel it going in and out while also cupping his hot balls. Then she whispered, "I want to 69 baby! I want to taste you. I want to feel your load slam against my throat like a battering ram. I want it so bad."

She had Aaron lay down on the floor and she straddled his head as she faced the other direction. She guided his member to her mouth as she wrapped her lips around it and seemed to savour its taste. As she took it deep into her mouth, she eased down on Aaron's mouth and he engulfed her throbbing womanhood which was dripping with desire.

The only sounds now were grunting and slurping sounds as they orally pleasured each other. Her juices were flowing like water from a tap, as it leaked into Aaron's mouth and coated his tongue. They were both moaning up a storm when Aaron felt the first tingling that signalled he was rapidly approaching the point of no return. He worked two fingers into her little brown pucker hole and drove them deep inside her as he felt her spasm slowly building.

She cried out as he worked both holes furiously, one with his mouth and the other with his fingers. Then Aaron was blasting a massive load of joy juice into her mouth and down her throat as she savoured every last drop. She was suddenly thrashing about on top of him, as she exploded with spasm after spasm of carnal euphoria. It felt like it started in her toes as Aaron felt them twitching, rushed up her spine and, then to her mound of desire straight into Aaron's waiting warm mouth.

They lay there exhausted, both swallowing, inhaling each others gratifying rapturous joy. Dripping wet with sweat, Myrna rolled off Aaron, her warm, hairy mound easing off his mouth as she released his now limp member from the warm embrace of her luscious lips.

"Wow," she muttered as she let out a sigh of exhaustive delight.

"Yeah," uttered Aaron. 'It seems that we figured out a way to ease our troubles a bit."

They almost doubled over in laughter, which turned to one last moan, as Aaron reached over and pulled her to his side on the floor that was moist with their sweat. Fornication had brought them great joy when they needed it most. Yes, sweet fornication had rendered two people a chance to reach for the nirvana of a moment in time when together they could enjoy the euphoric splendour of unbridled sexuality. Thus did the two share the great poetic essence of that which would relieve their sojourns through the corridors loneliness which had trapped them both in misery for so long.

The Girl Who Motivated Murder Most Foul

Erotic Manifestations: Two People in Search
Of Pleasure to Relieve the Pain of Loneliness

Come, Madam, come, all convention to defy,
Come by my side and erotically lie.
Memories of others will disappear from sight,
Do not this overwhelming desire fight.
Off with that gown, your skin is glistering,
And a tingling between the legs is encompassing.
Unpin that spangled bra which you wear,
That these eyes can longingly gaze there.
Unlace yourself, for that harmonious chime,
And know this is coupling time.

Your gown going off, such beauteous state reveals,
As when from that hairy mound my heart steals.
Now off with those shoes, and then safely tread
In this love's hallowed temple, this soft bed.
In such white robes, heaven's angels used to be
Received by my member; no angel now will be thee
Licence my roving hands, and let them go,
Before, behind, between, above, below.
Oh, you are gorgeous as my new-found-land,
Your kingdom, safest when you are with this man,
Your body is like precious stones, My Empire,
How blest am I in discovering thee!

To enter in these bonds, is to be free;
Then where my hand is set, my seal shall be.
Full nakedness! All joys are due to thee,
As souls unencumbered, bodies unclothed must be,

The Girl Who Motivated Murder Most Foul

To taste whole joys. Gems which you women use
Are like pearls cast into water wet with desire
That when a fool's eye lights on a gem,
My earthly soul may covet them.

Like pictures, or like books coverings made
For all-men, are all women thus arrayed;
They are mystic books, which only we
Whom their imputed grace will dignify
Must see revealed. Then since that I may know;
There is no penance due to innocence.
To teach thee, I am naked first; why then
Do you not join me in beloved lust.

Aaron and Myrna slept peacefully in each other's
that night, safe in the knowledge that they had found
a brief respite from the storms of dismay.

CHAPTER 9
DEATH WAS CALLING

Open the door.
Listen. Listen.
It is only the wind's muffled roar,
And the glisten
Of tears round the moon.
And in sweet fancy, the thread
Of misery is snapped.
There is a vanishing swoon
Out of the night.
Arise he who was long dead!

Hush, hush and hark!
To the sorrowful cry
Of the wind in the dark.
Hush, hush and hark,
Without a murmur or sigh.
Shed that binding thread,
That once bid you to die.
Hark, hark, hush and hark!

Aaron felt no remorse for sleeping with Myrna, because Jasmine had long ago decided to discard him for Brent. She had made the choice, not him. He actually felt exhilarated.

That morning, Aaron shared a glass of orange juice with Myrna. He tarried there because he felt comfortable for the first time in ages.

No, it was not love, only incredible lust. Yet, the two of them had managed to ease each others loneliness. A strange, beautiful feeling empowered Aaron; the certainty of being near an alluring woman titillated him. He enjoyed the scent of her hair; the warmth that irradiated from her body; the perfume of woman that accompanied her; the sweet breath every time she turned her face towards him, everything penetrated in an ungovernable way through all his senses. He reached across the able and touched her with his hand, passed his fingers over her shoulder, and smiled imbecilely like a teenager who had just got his first piece of ass.

He laughed at himself and asked if she wanted to walk to his office with him, maybe spend the day with him as he tried to piece together the puzzle of Denise's murder.

She agreed and they strolled through the snow laden city in relative silence, but they were both reflecting back over the incredible night they had spent together. A man passed them, with a pair of shoes under his arm; otherwise, the street was empty as far as they could see. Over at the Tivoli, a long row of lamps flickered off in unison to greet the day. It no longer was snowing; the sky was clear and although it was a bit chilly, the temperature was rather pleasant for a winter day. They looked at one another and smiled.

Aaron told her why he was investigating the death of Denise and began a long discourse on what happened. Despite some misgivings from Myrna, it was delightful to walk at her side and listen to her somewhat knowledgeable questions about the case.

They reached the fountains outside the entrance to Aaron's office. He stood there admiring her. For a woman of 55 she was remarkably attractive. This creature upset Aaron's chain of reasoning; turned it topsy-turvy. He was bewitched and extraordinarily happy. It seemed to him as if he were being dragged enchantingly into her lair. She reached toward him with her eyes, drew him to her by each word she spoke in sweet melodic rhapsody. He forgot for a moment his misery over losing Jasmine, his humble loneliness, his whole miserable condition. He felt his blood course madly through his whole body, as in the days when he was so in love with Jasmine, and resolved to rise like a mighty phoenix from the fires of hell to stand tall again as a man.

They began to laugh and jest; they talked incessantly as they stood in the cold. She told him that she knew he was right away the night before as she had seen his pictures in the papers many times over the years. She honestly had no intention of fornicating with him though, but she said she was pleased that it happened.

Aaron smiled and said, "Probably not as pleased as I am."

Again, they laughed together and Aaron invited her up to his office. After a morning in his office, Myrna said, "I must go Aaron, but will I see you again?"

Aaron immediately responded. "When and where?"

"Meet me here tomorrow tonight at 7. I will allow you to treat me to dinner."

Aaron enthusiastically replied, "Done, see you then."

She stretched herself up, flung her arms round Aaron's neck and kissed him passionately only once, swiftly, bewilderingly swiftly. He could feel how her bosom heaved; she was breathing violently. She wrenched herself suddenly out of his clasp, and almost breathlessly, almost whispering she turned and said, "I don't have time for that right now, but I promise it will happen again, and it will be even better than last night.

Aaron sighed and said, "That will be some feat. Last night was the wildest, greatest, most incredibly erotic night of my entire life, and I am no neophyte."

It snowed still more that day, a heavy snow mingled with rain; great wet flakes that fell to earth and were turned to mush from people trudging along the street. The air was raw and icy. Aaron sighed deeply and embraced the air, taking it in, filling his lungs with the city that never slept, the city that had captivated and imprisoned him in its strong arms that could either squeeze the life out of you or fill you with euphoria with its robust nature that could give you a sense of exhilaration for what it felt like to genuinely be alive. This was a city that could often alter between heaven and hell. Aaron had been in hell for so long that he thought he would never again rise from the depths of despair to which he had sunk since Jasmine left him, but the previous night in Myrna's arms had rejuvenated him, made him realize that when one door closes another often opens. He wasn't in love with Myrna, but she had showed him that there was still hope, even without Jasmine. However, he sensed that he could love Myrna. Yes, she was a fine woman, and with a smile slowly creeping across his lips he thought to himself – "and what a fuck!"

Strolling toward his office, he sensed that he was being followed. He looked behind him, but there was no one there. Yet, Aaron knew he was being tailed. So many years, so many incidents, so many cases had made him uniquely instinctive about things like that.

Aaron cut over to 44th street and went down Shepherd's Circle. He would double back and catch the bastard. The guy was really good – it didn't work. Aaron had walked the circle and assumed he would flush him out, but as he stood back at the entryway to the circular drive, he saw no one. He looked down in the snow and saw many footprints, so it was hard to distinguish which might be his. He noticed one set of prints that came to a halt and the person had turned and walked back to Broadway where the prints mingled with hundreds of others. This guy was a pro. It couldn't be Mr. McCord or either of his sons. They were too amateurish for this.

Aaron knew he was still out there. He could sense his prying eyes beaming in on him. Aaron scanned the street up and down, pausing to gaze into doorways, but there was nothing. Damn, this guy was not just good; he was an expert.

The sun was starting to go down. That would make it even harder to spot him once darkness descended on the city. Still, inside Aaron was feeling a sense of exhilaration. He loved the cat and mouse games of his profession. But who was it? He was on no case at present except for finding out who killed Denise. It wasn't the McCord's, but could it be someone they had hired? They were just stupid enough to put out a hit on Aaron. Yeah, they were the types who would go to a bank to get a loan to hire a hit man.

They were all gunning for Aaron, because each one of them thought it would be a boon to their family to have one of them married to Jasmine. These people were the kind who simply knew no boundaries when it came to protecting their kin, right or wrong. Brent was a fool, but his brother and father knew he was their fool, and they were prepared to do whatever it took to make this fool come on top in the battle against Aaron.

The thought of the previous evening's adventure crept into Aaron's mind as he scanned the street looking for the tail. What a wonderful feeling to once again experience the pleasure of a woman. OK, so he was technically married, but that had not kept Jasmine from fornicating with another man, so why should Aaron be hemmed in by convention? He was going to see Myrna again. Yes, she was a fine woman who aroused his manliness and he was looking forward to seeing her.

He wandered down the street, and swelled with satisfaction. His head was clear and buoyant. He felt inclined to take on this malevolent force that was tailing him. Little did he know that the tail was not just any ordinary person? Brent, his brother and father had pooled their resources and borrowed money to hire the best in the business.

The tail was not just assigned the job of following Aaron. He had been hired to kill him. Now, where did three malcontents like the McCord's get the money to hire a first class hit man? Simpletons can sometimes have contacts that would amaze you. These three men had an in-law named Hiram Netti, one of the city's premiere hit man who had been working for the Giovanni family for years. It just so happened that Hiram had married the senior McCord's much younger sister, and in the process became part of a circle of fools that made up this family of malcontents. He owed them a favour, because they had agreed to keep a secret. The secret was that the three knew he had a mistress he kept in a Manhattan high rise. So, he was basically blackmailed into eliminating Aaron Adams for a mere $100,000. Yet, it was a chore he would enjoy, as he took great pride in being a man who went up against the best and came out on top. Doing Aaron would actually be a feather in his cap.

The night crawled slowly by like a wounded snake and Aaron contemplated his meandering life that had been up and down like a rollercoaster for some time. He went home, crawled into bed and put the worries over the tail out of his mind as he drifted off to sleep. The morning greeted him with a dingy grey that was varnishing the sky. The cry of the city that never slept drifted through the walls as he prepared his morning coffee.

There was something in the air, something that seemed to penetrate Aaron's brain and heighten the senses. As he shaved, showered and dressed, the hairs on the back of his neck were prickly. His breathing was slow and laboured. He looked in the mirror and told himself that something was up; something big was going to happen this day.

He decided to confront Brent that morning. As he left his co-op, he felt, but did not see, the presence of that most intrepid of pursuers. He could not see him, but knew he was there. It did not matter, because it was daylight, and this person was too much of a professional to take on Aaron in the daytime. This person would work under the cover of darkness. Then as quickly as a flash of lightning, his tail was gone. Aaron did not see him drop off the chase, but he felt it. The man was gone, apparently deciding to return to his lair, rest and prepare for the coming battle. Deep inside, Aaron was feeling almost euphoric over the coming battle. It was causing his blood to course through his veins faster and the nitrogen bubbles in his brain were giving him a "high." Yet, who was this person? Why was he tailing Aaron? There was only one answer. He had to be connected to the McCord's.

The showdown was coming soon. Like the old western movies, high noon was on its way, slowly ticking toward the ultimate confrontation.

Brent's job site was near Aaron's office. Aaron walked into the main reception area and asked if he could see Brent who was busy sweeping the floors of debris. Brent and Aaron had been together before, but only in the presence of Jasmine. Brent always put up a great façade to appear meek and kind to Aaron. Yet, Aaron, unlike Jasmine, could read beneath the surface, seeing the seething anger within Brent. The eyes, it is said, are windows to the soul. If that were the case, Brent's soul was pure evil, as you could sense that there was intense anger toward Aaron for being far more intelligent, more articulate, more respected, more in control of his finances and better, despite Jasmine's betrayal of him, able to make Jasmine see the reality of situations rather than just act on impulse as Brent did.

Aaron had learned to recognize the thorough and primitive duality of man. The real Brent McCord was a second form hidden within under his good old boy facade and a countenance substituted that bore the stamp, of the lower elements of a soul that was pure evil. Thus, Brent was two equipotent, coexistent, and eternally opposed components of a man that made him different than the normal individual. In him, good and evil were not related but were two independent entities, individuals even, different in mental and physical attributes and constantly at war with each other. Evil does not require the existence of good to justify itself but it exists simply as itself, depicted as being the more powerful, the more enjoyable of the two, and in the end ultimately it is the one that controlled Brent's thoughts. Aaron recognized the phases of Brent's lucidity of evil as a real danger to Jasmine. Aaron's perception went beyond the fact that this man had stolen his wife, because Aaron had already accepted the fact that she was gone, but that fact could not keep him from trying to make her see that this man was not in love with her, but in love with the idea of having her love him. His ego craved her, made the possession of her the centre of his existence.

Brent came through the swinging doors to the reception area with an arrogant swagger as his massive, tree trunk size arms swayed from side to side and his eyes stared at Aaron like a piercing laser. Aaron thought to himself that this was man capable of extreme violence and that if he could get away with it, he would have no compunction whatsoever in killing Aaron. Aaron was the one thing that stood between him and what he wanted more than anything else in the world. Brent's ego simply could never let Jasmine go. That would be too big a blow to endure.

Without Jasmine present, Brent felt emboldened and let down his façade of kindness. "What the hell you want Aaron? Get used to the fact she loves me, not you."

Aaron, very calmly replied, "I just want to let you know a few things Brent. That's all. You see, you are going to need a good lawyer, because I am going to prove you killed Denise. You represent the kind of evil that is the most perverse. You put up this good old boy façade that fools most people, but I am not fooled in the least bit. I can see into your soul. I know how empty of compassion you are inside. You have love for nothing or nobody but your family. Your family is your refuge from the hatred that possesses you. You actually hate yourself, because you see yourself as the supreme loser, a man who has a past that bespeaks of sinister disregard for your responsibilities as a son, a husband and a father. You think you are a man of integrity, but inside you know that you have no core, no real belief in anything that truly matters. You are barren inside, empty, lost in a burning self-emollition that is devouring your soul. You think that Jasmine can assuage your misery and make you whole once you possess her, but nothing you do will ever compensate for the evil that consumes you. I am bringing you down, not because I hate you, but because I hate what you do to people. I hate the monstrous way you have tried to control a woman who is as vulnerable as a small child. I hate the way you think you have a right to kill someone you deem an abomination. Most of all I hate you for the unmitigated façade you put up to fool so many people who fall for your deceptions."

The receptionist was standing behind the counter listening intently to the conversation. Aaron looked over at her, smiled, turned back to Brent and continued. "You are scared. You don't want to admit it, but you are scared that people will one day see the real you, the person you keep hidden deep within. You live a lie, and you know I can see the truth. That galls you so much that you and, I guess, your brother and father have hired an assassin who is tailing me and waiting for the right moment to eliminate me. Tell him to be very careful, because he, and you Brent, have never gone up against a man like me. You see, I know what I am capable off, and I know what is at my core. I am a good and kind man, but I am also an avenging angel, because when I see evil I confront it. I see the evil within you, and I warn you to be eternally vigilant, because I am not Denise. I am not going to be so easy to kill. Tell that to your assassin, and tell him that I am waiting. In fact, I am eagerly waiting. Bring it on asshole."

Brent was breathing heavily, and the words came with great difficulty. His massive arms were pulsating and the veins beginning to bulge. "OK asshole. You are fucking with the wrong man. I am afraid of nobody, especially an old, decrepit man like you. You are going to fall hard asshole."

Smiling, Aaron replied "If I fall, you'll go down with me and it won't be pleasant."

Brent, arrogantly replied, "She loves me asshole, not you. It galls you that she could love a man like me. You just can't understand it."

"Brent, I can understand it. You got a big cock and mine has shrivelled with years. You excite her with your good old boy façade and fantastic fornicating. You have fooled her, but you have not fooled me. I know the real you, and that galls the hell out of you. I know you are a little boy in a man's body. You have spent your life living for the here and now with no thought of tomorrow. Your life is about instant gratification. You always thought that no woman of real quality and class would have anything to do with you. Now, you have snared that kind of woman and you can't bear the thought of letting her go, because it would be too big a blow to your ego. This whole affair is about you, and your egocentricity. You see Jasmine as your last chance to make yourself feel worthwhile. She offers ego gratification that you never dreamed possible. You want the world to know that you are important, that you are somebody. You can only prove that with Jasmine. You will never let her go. I know that, but when you are in jail for murder getting rammed in the rear by a hot stud, believe me, you will finally be somebody. You will be somebody's bitch."

Brent was seething with anger. "You bastard. You….."

Before he could get another word out, Aaron turned and said as he left, "You've got nothing I want to hear asshole. Tell it to your friend behind the counter there, who knows what you are all about now, and will tell your co-workers that Aaron Adams put you in your place and laid your soul bare. You can drop your façade in front of them now and let that little scared boy come out from inside and cry for his mommy."

Aaron walked through the outer door into the cold air, took a deep breath and felt good. He got into his car, pulled onto the street and noticed a brown sedan following him. OK thought Aaron, now I'll take care of this bastard too.

As he turned onto 48th Street, he thought he would lure the guy into a parking arcade and then take him on. He turned into an underground arcade, but the guy kept going. Smart thought Aaron. He was going to pick the time and place, not Aaron. Yeah, this guy was a pro.

Aaron started thinking about Myrna, got a little tingle between his legs and headed over to her apartment. He parked around the corner from her place just to be safe. The tail was no where in sight, but just to be extra careful he walked two blocks away from Myrna's and then doubled back. He was sure he wasn't being tailed, so he went to Myrna's place feeling confident that no one was following him.

It does not matter how good you are at something. There is always someone better than you are. Aaron had gone up against the well known Egyptian assassin, El Rausuli, many years before, and only came out on top because his beloved secretary B.J. had come to his rescue. He should have died then and there, but he managed to survive thanks to her courage. Then there was the Mafia hit man Fluke Williams whom he left in a trash can off 43rd Street. Don McBride was a Detroit hit man brought in especially to take him out. Aaron had actually toyed with him before dispatching him. Then there were the two assassins who had gone up against him when he was rescuing Jasmine Alexander. Yeah, the *Whirlwind* was probably the best of them all. Still, Aaron had managed to survive in a face-off with him. Hell, this guy couldn't be better than any of them! Unfortunately, this one might not have been better, but he was more adapt at keeping out of sight, which would lead to catastrophic circumstances.

As he walked in the cold toward Myrna's, there was a buzzing in his ears, and intoxication over the fantastic sex they had ran riot in his brains. He distinguished every nuance in the voice and laughter of the passers-by, observed some pigeons that hopped before him in the street, took to studying the designs of the paving-stones that peeped through the snow, and discovered all sorts of tokens and signs in them. Thus occupied, he arrived at Lynton Place. He stood stock-still, and looked at a bronze plaque commemorating the end of World War II on a building and thought how wars were mostly fought to enrich the wealthy more than secure democracy. For many years Americans had fallen for the corporate and government propaganda that exalted and praised the military and how it was protecting America. Yeah thought Aaron, it was protecting capitalism and the exploitation of third world countries by corporations. Americans were too stupid to realize that they were not free as long as they had to live pay check to pay check, go without free healthcare, spend lavishly on the military while ignoring education and a host of other social needs, bow to corporations that controlled their lives, and the one that galled Aaron the most – how can you be free when you have religion shoved down your throat constantly. Religion and America were one and the same, and America had gone across the world under the leadership of the biggest buffoon to ever inhabit the White House to fight against the Taliban while the fundamentalist Christians wanted the same thing for the USA, only they wanted Jesus to be exalted rather than Mohammad. Yeah, even in World War II, the industrialists and bankers kept doing business with Hitler until the government finally forced them as a result of pressure from France and Britain to stop trading with Germany. The driving force in America was not democracy but the dollar.

People were wandering about, chatting and laughing in the bitter weather. Aaron felt uneasy, so he hailed a cab and decided to go for a little ride just to make sure he wasn't being tailed. "Just drive around for awhile cabbie. I'll tell you where to let me out."

On the way the driver looked round, stooped and peeped with his peripheral vision at Aaron. He was obviously apprehensive of Aaron. "Hey man, what you up to?"

"I am just making sure I am not being tailed. I am a P.I., don't be alarmed." Aaron took out his licence and reached over the back of the seat and flashed it for the cabbie to peruse.

"OK dude. It is just that I been robbed so many times I have to be careful."

"I understand. Too bad they rob the cabbies and the clerks at 7/11 when they should be robbing the barons of Wall Street."

Laughing, the cabbie said, "You got that right mister. I work my ass off and make in a month what those bastards make in a day. Damn shame!"

Aaron, feeling philosophical said, "Well, as long as we let them get a way with it they will. Politicians aren't going to stop it, because they are part of the problem. When all the poor people march on Wall Street and smash their kingdom, then we will all be really free. Unfortunately, that is not going to happen – too much complacency and the police are part of their empire. That's why they pay them so well, to keep the rest of us in line."

"Damn man. You sound like an anarchist."

"No, just a man who sees suffering and wants to heal it. I see inequity and want to end it, and I know that power does not transfer to the meek. It comes to those who are willing to resort to violence in order to achieve what they want. This country was founded on violence – violence against England. Without that violent upheaval, England would still be here today. You don't get what you want by meekly begging the powerful and wealthy to please give you your fair share. Those guys who flew the planes into the World Trade Centre knew that no amount of begging for justice would get them a hearing before the high and mighty in America who always side with the moneyed interests. They resorted to violence, because they saw that it worked for the USA, as whenever it didn't get what it wanted the military option was exercised with great efficiency."

The driver, who was obviously Pakistani, and therefore, likely a Muslim, said, "Damn, you don't sound like the typical American. You understand things better than most."

"I understand that this nation is an impediment to peace, because it will not let other people solve their own problems. When Dwight Eisenhower left the presidency in 1960, he warned of the growing influence of the military-industrial complex and how it would lead this nation into endless conflicts to fuel an economy dependent on war. He was a general in World War II who knew that this nation had created a monster, and that monster would devour everything in its sight to satisfy its avaricious greed."

Impressed, the cabbie said, as Aaron signalled for him to pull over, "Man, I'd like to have you speak at our mosque."

Aaron replied, "Mosque, Synagogue, temple, church – they are all the same – fairy tales to keep people in bondage. Stop here. I need to get out."

The driver pulled to the curb. Aaron handed him two twenties and said, "Keep the change." He looked around the street as the driver pulled away and saw no signs of a tail. He turned back toward Myrna's place and began the two kilometre walk as light snow begin to fall again.

In measure, Aaron walked on, and began to feel languid and weary. The snow was now falling in great moist flakes. He began to see phantoms all about as dark shadows danced against the walls of buildings. Was the heavy load of his misery returning to weigh him down once again with sorrow?

As he got nearer and nearer to Myrna's, he had the half-conscious feeling of approaching something dangerous, but he determined to stick to his purpose, because he knew that the tail was not there. Nobody was that good. Nobody could completely hide from Aaron Adams no matter how professional he was.

All at once visions of Myrna danced in his head. Light forced its way ever so faintly into his spirit again, a little ray of sunshine that made him warm inside; and gradually more light came, a rare, silken, balmy light that caressed him with soothing loveliness. And the brightness inside him grew stronger and stronger, burning sharply in his temples as it spread throughout his body. Then, suddenly a maddening pyre of rays flamed up before his eyes; a heaven and earth in conflagration with men and beasts of fire, mountains of fire, devils of fire, an abyss, a wilderness, a hurricane, a universe in brazen ignition, a smoking, smouldering caldron of evil that wanted to embrace him.

His heart raced furiously and he turned quickly to look behind him, then right, and then left, then straight ahead. Damn, the tail had him spooked. Even when he wasn't there, he had Aaron thinking he was there. This guy was good, maybe the best!

Finally, he was there. Myrna opened the door and a big smile crept across her face. She did not know that death was calling.

CHAPTER 10
WHEN THEY SHIP YOU TO SING-SING

From the depths of hell rises evil,
A mighty devil takes on human form
Like a phantom ascending from the sea.
Terrorizing the fragile mind,
He is a vassal for those
Who have hearts of stone.
He is but an instrument of hostility;
A merciless turbulence that spits fire.

He steals all hope in the night,
His gust of rage roars like rolling thunder,
He is the evil knight of darkness
That razes hope with murderous glee.
A mighty tempest is he.
A disgrace to humanity
That robs life and steals with impunity.
Evil is his mantra and cloak.

Engraving echoes of tears
Brings him great delight.
Vain, wicked, and devoid of compassion
He steals life and laughs.
The pain he dispenses
Is the nourishment of his soul.
Among the sands of time
His evil is measured grain by grain.
Tarry not in his presence
Because he spits fire!

Fornication is as natural as the desire to eat, and Aaron and Myrna savoured a banquet of delight that night in each other's arms, but deep within they both carried the heavy baggage of hearts broken by the ones they truly loved. They found solace in each other's arms, but they still had that hollowness inside as they were trapped in an inferno of what was rather than thoughts of what might be. There's was a journey of lost hope, and they could not embrace wholeheartedly the sunshine that could warm and nurture them through their pain.

Aaron turned to her as she lay in his arms and whispered softly "Myrna, you made me dizzy and so confused about things. I am at home in your arms. I feel that you are a safe harbour from that which afflicts me."

She smiled as he continued. "The light in this room seems to bathe you with serenity as you lie so still. For me, you are a tree that stands in stormy winds and gusts, causing the fabric of my soul to be soothed. Your long limbs held with such grace, makes you seem so alluring. Your delicate nose framed beautifully by your porcelain cheeks, your lips so succulent like the intricately placed thorn on a rose, beautiful and sharp, titillate me with desire. Like a river snaking down a mountain, you are cool and quench my thirst for hope at a time when I feel lost."

Myrna, overwhelmed at Aaron's glowing rendition, snuggled up to him closer and said, "Go on Mr. Poetic. I love it."

"Your aura caresses me the like a river shapes a canyon. You pull on me the way the moon pulls on the tranquil night time seas. Your eyes pierce me, there's something there, something darker, masked by a beauty that seems almost too restrained. Your eyes captivate and enthral me. They bore through me and it fills me with an inescapable feeling that surrounds me and bears down on my soul. Ah, and your smell is like the calm before the storm. There is a passion deep within you that boils to the surface and rages with desire. Tonight our sex was more restrained than the first time we met, but it was no less intense. You stoke the fires of passion within me, and I feel so comfortable in your arms. Yet, I must confess I sense that your heart still belongs to another as does mine. Are we just two ships passing in the night or are we going to be more than two people wallowing in misery who find solace in each other's arms?"

Myrna softly replied, "I don't know Aaron. All I know is that I am at peace for the first time in ages. I know that when I am in your arms I feel whole again. Is it just sex or something much deeper? I know you are asking yourself the same question. Only time will tell."

Aaron and Myrna made love. As she got up and asked if he wanted something to eat, Aaron smiled and said, "Myrna, let's go out for a bite."

She motioned toward the shower and said, "me or you first?"

"Together," said Aaron with a devilish smile.

After showering, they strolled outside and headed toward a diner around the corner. The hairs on the back of Aaron's neck bristled, and he turned to see if someone was following them. I am paranoid he thought, just paranoid. Like America thinking that everyone is out to get it, I think that the pro is always there, always looking to do me harm. He wouldn't dare do it with so many people still on the streets. Yeah, he and Myrna were safe.

They had a leisurely meal and shared laughter. They were growing especially fond of each other and Aaron began to think to himself, "Was there life after Jasmine?"

She invited him to spend the night, but Aaron had a big day tomorrow, and he said he would get no sleep next to Myrna. She laughed and said "My door's always open to you Aaron Adams. Remember that."

Aaron smiled, winked at her and walked away.

He strolled along the sidewalk toward Bryon Park. There was a short cut through the park, so he crossed the street and walked through the darkness and fog that made the park seem foreboding. Light snow flurries were falling, and he heard the sound of footsteps crunching the snow far behind him.

Something was coming through the snow toward him, coming slowly, carefully, coming by the same winding way he had come. He moved into the brush and leaned against a tree. Through a screen of brush almost as thick as tapestry, he watched for whatever it was following him.

He could not see him, only sense him. He was there in the fog and snow, heard but not seen. Aaron's eyes were fixed in utmost concentration on the area before him. He could hear the figure beneath the trees, moving slowly as if surveying the ground. Aaron's impulse was to hurl himself out in the open like a panther, but he knew he was at a disadvantage, because he wasn't sure of the man's location.

The hunter of humans, unseen and unbeknownst to Aaron, shook his head several times in the fog and snow as if he was puzzled. Then he straightened up and took from his inside pocket a Lugar pistol he had used for years as his weapon of destruction. He stood there fingering it, relishing the coming kill.

Aaron slowed his breathing for fear he might be heard. Meanwhile, Hiram Netti's eyes were scanning the nearby brush hiding Aaron. Aaron froze there, every muscle tensed for a spring if Netti appeared.

But the sharp eyes of the hunter stopped and focued on the area where he sensed Aaron was. A smile spread over his deeply furrowed face. Very deliberately he whispered in the fog: "Your advantage now Adams, but be aware it is coming soon."

Then Netti turned and walked defiantly away, assured that he had the upper hand. He walked back along the trail he had come. The crunching of the snow under his feet grew fainter and fainter.

The pent-up air burst hotly from Aaron's lungs. His first thought made him feel sick and numb. This guy was really good and could follow him almost undetected. He must have uncanny powers; only by the merest chance had Aaron avoided death. Why had the assassin turned back? Because he was smart, so smart he wasn't taking the slightest chance. He had not known Aaron's exact location because of the fog, and he was too canny to take the risk. Yes, this guy was a real pro.

Aaron did not want to believe what his reason told him was true, but the truth was as evident as the moon that had by now pushed through the darkness. The assassin was playing with him! He was saving him for another day's sport! The assassin was the cat; Aaron was the mouse. Then it was that Aaron knew the full meaning of terror that could be inflicted by one person on another. This was more than an assassination. It was a just an assassination to this killer, yes, it was a game of cat and mouse.

Aaron struck off through the park. His face was set and he forced the machinery of his mind to function. Three hundred metres from his hiding place he stopped where a huge dead tree leaned precariously on a smaller, living one, because ultimately this was not over. He knew that the assassin would be waiting for him at the far exit from the park. No need to turn around thought Aaron, because the confrontation was inevitable, and now was as good a time as any to confront the bastard.

Aaron thought to himself that this would probably be a close quarter's confrontation. This guy probably liked to be close when he made a kill.

Aaron took out his knife from its sheath inside his right breast pocket and began to work with all his energy. The job was finished in a few minutes, and he threw himself down behind a fallen limb a hundred metres away. He did not have to wait long. The cat was coming again to play with the mouse.

Following the trail with the sureness of a bloodhound came Netti. Nothing escaped those searching dark eyes, no crushed piece of snow, no bent twig, no mark, no matter how faint, in the snow. So intent was Netti on his stalking that he was upon the thing Aaron had made before he saw it. His foot touched the protruding bough that was the trigger. Even as he touched it, Netti sensed his danger and leaped back with great agility. But he was not quite quick enough; the dead tree, delicately adjusted to rest on the cut living one, crashed down and struck him a glancing blow on the shoulder as it fell; but for his alertness, he would have been smashed beneath it. He staggered, but he did not fall; nor did he drop his drawn revolver. He stood there, rubbing his injured shoulder, and Aaron, with the death dealing 45 in his hand, heard Netti mockingly laugh. He wanted to squeeze off a round in the direction of the laugh, but feared someone else might be coming through the park who could be hit with a stray bullet.

"Adams" called Netti, "if you are within the sound of my voice, as I suppose you are, let me congratulate you. Not many men know how to make a VC man-catcher. Luckily for me I, too, have been in Vietnam. You are proving interesting, Mr. Adams. I am going now to have my wound dressed; it's only a slight one. But I shall confront you again. I am enjoying this."

Aaron was careful leaving the park, but suspected that the assassin, whose name he still did not know, was long gone and was licking his wounds, preparing for another confrontation in the near future. Aaron left the park, knowing that he was safe for awhile from the assassin, but how long he did not know. He thought about Jasmine and Myrna. Loving Jasmine had been incredibly costly. It was beyond the realm of his understanding why he had to pay such a high price for loving her, but now there was Myrna, and she had made him realize that sometimes, when you least expect it, something good comes into your life.

Aaron was going to take out Netti, but first he had to bring down Brent. Yes, he was going to bring Brent to justice for the murder of Denise as the day before he had brought in Brent's shirt from Jasmine's cabin to have it analyzed for a very important reason. Aaron had told John Havoc the details that would lead to Brent being charged with murder. It was obvious to Johnny that Aaron had solved the case. He made a call to the sheriff in Finger Lakes. He and Aaron waited. They were going over to arrest Brent when the sheriff arrived.

It was 12:00 PM when the sheriff arrived and an arrest warrant had already been issued from through the Finger Lakes County Court and forwarded to the Manhattan District Court where a judge issued it without any haste. The three men went to Brent's workplace. When Brent walked out from the shop floor, he was shocked to see all three men present. On his face was a look of disbelief. He simply could not comprehend what was happening.

Johnny Havoc said, "Brent C. McCord, you are under arrest for the murder of Denise Colman, you have a right to remain silent. Anything you say can and will be used against in a court of law. You are entitled to an attorney, and if you cannot afford one, one will be appointed for you. I read from the warrant issued by the Manhattan Superior Court as requested by the Yates County District Attorney as follows: *You are commanded to arrest and bring before the magistrate of Manhattan District Court for transfer to the Yates County District Court, Brent C. McCord, without necessary delay, who is accused of an offence or violation based on the following document filed with the court: Indictment for murder in the First Degree by the Yates County District Attorney's office.* Now, please turn around and place your hands behind your back."

Brent was in such a state of shock, he shook. As

he turned around he said, "Fuck you Adams. This isn't going to work. There is no evidence whatsoever connecting me to this crime."

Aaron smiling broadly said, "Brent, you forgot one very important thing when you tossed her over the edge of the cliff. That one thing is what did you in, buddy. Denise was transgendered, and she had saline breast implants. You hated her for being different. That and the fact she was calling me to tell me what was going on between you and Jasmine is what got her killed. You dropped the body on the rocks, so you could get a better grip before tossing her over. You picked her up over your head and the puncture in her breast implants dripped down on the shoulder of your shirt. You see, when I was at Jasmine's I took the shirt you had on the day of the crime as you left clothes there for your weekend fornicating escapades. I handed it over to Johnny, and he had it analyzed. There was saline solution on it. That is going to be very difficult to refute. Gotcha asshole."

Brent was raging angry now and tried lunging for Aaron, who just stepped back and kept smiling. Brent was literally writhing with anger, even foaming at the mouth and shaking violently. The sheriff, Havoc and two uniformed policeman restrained him and headed out the door with him in tow. Brent looked back at Aaron and said, "You're still dead asshole. Still dead!!"

Aaron couldn't resist one last jab at the homophobic Brent, "I'll get you some lube as a going away present when they ship you to Sing - Sing."

CHAPTER 11
AND EMBRACED ETERNITY

It is not our part to master
all the tides of the world,
but to do what is in us
for the succour of those years
wherein we are here,
uprooting the evil in the fields
that we know to protect
those we love.
We must till the soil of hope
and let good crops
rise from the earth
so that those who live after
may have clean earth to till.
Do not fear evil.
Fight it with all your might.
In the end the righteous man
will stand triumphant
before the throne of love.

Aaron called Jasmine with the news of Brent's arrest and she broke down in tears, but admitted that she suspected Aaron was right all alone about him killing Denise. However, she was reluctant to confirm it, because she loved Brent so much that she could not see through the façade he used as a manipulative tool to enthral her. She was not angry with Aaron, because she knew that he uncovered the truth, not because he hated Brent, but because he loved her and wanted what was best for her, even if it did not include him. They talked for over three hours, and by the time the conversation ended, they were laughing and planning on seeing each other soon.

Now, Aaron had seen Myrna only three times but he did have feelings for her, because she had brought him comfort when he desperately needed it. Of course, he too, had brought joy into her life when she was crying in the wilderness of despair. He was on his way to see her to let her know what had happened in regards to Brent. His cell-phone rang. "Hello."

"Adams, this is your nemesis. You might think that the arrest of Brent McCord brings an end to your troubles, but I was paid to do a job, and like you, I am a man of my word."

Aaron, not surprised at Netti's devotion to his work, replied "I can appreciate that, but I see no need for us to tangle when Brent is in jail, and will be spending, my guess is, 25 years to life up the river. I have no animosity toward you for the other night. Let's call it a day and go about our business."

"I thought you would say that. In fact, I asked myself how could I get this guy to go one-on-one. Know what I came up with?"

Aaron, growing weary of the banter, said with a bit of trepidation, "No, what did you come up with?"

"Well, I know you like a lady named Myrna. So, you see, I kidnapped her and brought her to a nice little place outside the city. Go ahead, call and check. I had her leave you a message on her answering machine. I'll give you three minutes, and then I'll call you back with details on how we are going to settle this little matter between us."

Aaron hung up immediately and called Myrna. The message sent a chill through him. "Aaron, this is Myrna. It's true. Do what he says."

Aaron waited frantically for the call. He was prompt. "OK Adams, so just follow my direction precisely and she may live, if you kill me that is."

"I won't only kill you. I'll rip out your heart while you are still alive."

A sinister laugh from Netti let Aaron know that he was not just going up against a man who was a professional, but one who thoroughly enjoyed his work. This bastard enjoyed killing, and he had Myrna. "Drive across the George Washington Bridge to the New Jersey Turnpike. Get on it in Fort Lee. Drive until you come to the Secaucus Exit, when you get off follow the signs to town. A billboard will have a partially dressed baby on it with the words *Get a Coppertone Tan*. Take a right onto McNair Road after the sign. Follow it until you come to a crossroads. Make a left, park your car and walk into the forest. I'll be waiting for you. Notify the authorities and she is dead."

Aaron, leery, said "How do I know you haven't already killed her?"

Again, there was a sinister laugh. "You don't."

What choice did he have? Aaron hung up and headed for the G.W. and the Jersey Pike.

Hiram Netti was a man obsessed. His mannerisms were refined and elegant. In fact, he was probably a man out of his time, as he should have been born in the 19th century. He seemed a cultured man, but his refinement and cultural manifestations concealed a maniacal desire to inflict suffering and death for his own amusement. He loved playing God. The power over life and death made him feel exhilarated. His killing skills were developed and honed by that most efficient training ground for murderers – the U.S. Army. He learned to hate all who were not American, because they somehow seemed less human. Yet, he also enjoyed killing Americans when he got out of the army, because life to him was nothing more than a game of survival for the fittest.

He was truly quiet mad and his inflated ego was stoked like a raging fire when he was able to somehow play games with his victims. He had learned to be an assassin in the army, and he was so good at his work that his superiors began to fear he could not be controlled as he enjoyed his work so much. He commanded a group of soldiers who idolized him for his bravery and coldness. He actually loved the horrors and atrocities of warfare. His bloodlust and passion for killing eventually prompted him to hunt men as a profession as he found them the most cunning and challenging prey he could find. Going up against the best was an inducement that made the whole process about more than just money.

Accustomed to death, Netti lost the ability to distinguish men from beasts as he became barbaric and uncaring. The sanctioned violence of his profession drained him of any empathy and he lacked the capacity to make moral judgments. His passion for the hunt of his prey and devaluation of human life made him uniquely suited for his profession.

On the other end of the spectrum was Aaron Adams, a man of deep moral fibre, empathy with the downtrodden and dedicated to fighting evil, especially the evil of capitalism with all his glorification of greed. Yet, he was capable of using violence in defence of righteousness, and he had killed, but never without just cause.

Aaron drove down the dark road toward the forest, knowing that he was going up against evil of the vilest kind. Oh, how he wished he had never gone home with Myrna.

Parking his car as instructed, Aaron sat and waited for the inevitable phone call. *"Throw your gun across the road. I can see you. You don't do as I say, she dies. After tossing your gun, proceed into the forest on your right. There is a pathway. It will be easy to follow. It will lead you to Myrna. Prepare for some fun Mr. Adams. By the way, I want to introduce myself before the game begins. I am Hiram Netti."*

The name did not strike fear into Aaron, but he knew the name well. He had been implicated in many murders, but never convicted. He was a man with connections and a man known to all as one who liked toying with his prey. Aaron walked through the darkness, not wanting to use the pen light on his key chain, because he knew that no matter how good Netti was, that the night prevented him from knowing exactly where Aaron was in the darkness.

The moon was in its quarter phase and cast a dimmed, eerie glow on the pathway. How Aaron wished there was no moon, because as he came to a clearing, the moon danced a light of sinister intent as he gazed upon a sight that brought heart-wrenching pain as he had never experienced before. There, hanging in the clearing swaying back and forth in the gentle breeze dangled the body of Myrna who had been hanged from the limb of a giant oak tree. There was no need to check. She was dead. She had paid the extreme price for simply knowing Aaron. He seethed with indignant anger and whispered to himself, "Hiram Netti will pay dearly for this."

Aaron eased back into the forest, knowing that if he stepped into the moonlit clearing that Netti had the advantage. He turned and headed back toward his car. It was flight now, a desperate, hopeless flight that carried him on for a few minutes. The ground grew softer under his feet; the vegetation grew ranker, denser; insects bit him savagely. Somehow, he had gotten lost.

He stepped forward; his foot sank into the ooze. He tried to wrench it back, but the muck sucked viciously at his foot as if it were a giant leech. With a violent effort, he tore his foot loose. He knew where he was now. He was in the New Jersey swampland which was filled with quicksand.

His hands were tightly closed as if his nerves were something tangible that someone in the darkness was trying to tear from his grip. The softness of the earth had given him an idea. He stepped back from the quicksand a dozen feet or so and he began to dig.

Aaron understood the mentality of the pursuer. He was a man who enjoyed the chase more than the killing of his prey. He dug furiously. The pit grew deeper; when it was above his shoulders, he climbed out and from some hard saplings cut stakes with his pocket knife and sharpened them to a fine point. These stakes he planted in the bottom of the pit with the points sticking up. The Viet Cong had used this method to kill American soldiers. It was one way they defeated the greatest military power in the world. No matter how powerful an enemy is, he can be defeated with wiliness, determination, courage and dedication to a cause you know is just. With flying fingers he wove a rough carpet of weeds and branches and with it he covered the mouth of the pit. Then, wet with sweat and aching with tiredness, he crouched behind a nearby tree and waited.

He knew his pursuer was coming; he heard the padding sound of feet on the soft earth. It seemed to Aaron that Netti was coming with unusual swiftness; he was not feeling his way along, foot by foot. Crouching there he had visions of Myrna dancing in his head and tears formed in his eyes. He lived a year in a minute. Then he felt an impulse to cry aloud with joy, for he heard the sharp crackle of the breaking branches as the cover of the pit gave way; he heard the sharp scream of pain as the pointed stakes found their mark. He leaped up from his place of concealment. Then he immediately dropped to the ground again as a shot rang out and a bullet buried itself into the tree he was using for cover. He rolled over and over into the thicket as a voice shouted "You've done well, Aaron. Your VC tiger pit was ingenious. That is why I thought I'd fake a scream and make you think it was successful. Touché my friend. Touché! I am coming for you Adams. You are a dead man, but just don't know it yet."

Aaron knew he could do one of two things. He could stay where he was and wait. That was suicide. He could flee. That was postponing the inevitable. For a moment he lay there, thinking. An idea that held a wild chance came to him, and, tightening his belt, he headed away from the swamp, crawling on his stomach.

He crawled to a nearby ridge and climbed a tree. The slight light of the moon let him see far into the distance, maybe at least two or three hundred metres. Down below in the far distance, he could see the brush moving. Straining his eyes, he saw the lean figure of Netti as his wide shoulders surged through the tall weeds. However, it was the unseen that worried Aaron the most. He was carrying in his right hand, not a rifle, as that was slung over his left shoulder, but a Samurai sword. He intended killing Aaron close up. He was going to disembowel him, make him suffer excruciating pain.

Netti would be on him any minute now. His mind worked frantically. He thought of a trick he had learned in Vietnam from the greatest, most wily and determined fighters the world had ever gone up against. He slid down the tree. He caught hold of a springy young sapling and to it he fastened his pocket knife, with the blade pointing down the trail; with a bit of wild grapevine he tied back the sapling. Then he ran for his life like a wild animal. Hell, he thought, men are animals. Why shouldn't I act like one to survive, because Netti is acting like one as he pursues me. No, no Netti was not acting like an animal. An animal dispenses of its prey swiftly, but Netti was a man, and men were worse than animals on so many levels.

He stopped to catch his breath. The whole forest was deathly quiet. Surely Netti must have reached the knife.

Aaron shimmied excitedly up a tree and looked back. His pursuer had stopped. But the hope that was in Aaron's brain when he climbed died, for he saw as he looked at the shallow valley Netti was still alive. However, the knife, driven by the recoil of the springing tree, had not wholly failed. Netti had tumbled to the ground and lay there as he pulled the knife from his right shoulder. He was still breathing and now Aaron was without any weapon at all.

"He is good, maybe the best," Aaron muttered to himself. There was a gap between the trees dead ahead and across from the clearing he could see a cabin. There was a light on, but Aaron did not want to threaten the safety of whoever was in the cabin. Netti had already killed one innocent person, and Aaron did not want the blood of another innocent on his hands. He turned to his left and headed into a thicket, purposefully breaking branches to make sure Netti could easily follow him; thereby, making sure he did not go to the cabin and needlessly kill another innocent person.

Aaron came upon a large pond and pondered for a moment, reflecting back on the night he and Jasmine Alexander went up against two assassins in Europe. Ah, she was his strong ally that night. Without her, he would be dead. Now, because of her, he was facing death again.

As Aaron contemplated, Netti was standing nearby cleverly examining the situation. He took a seat on the ground, shrugged his shoulders and contemplated the situation. He was thinking to himself, "This guy is the best I have ever gone up against. I should have just shot him when I had the chance."

He scanned the horizon and could not see Aaron. A bit of fright edged its way into his psyche. Where was he?

Aaron was moist all over, his whole body bathed in dampness. The fear was there, but it did not overwhelm him. He looked about in amazement and felt a complete transformation of his being. He felt along his arms and down his legs, and was struck with astonishment that he was whole. His hair clung wet and cold about his forehead. He raised himself on his elbow and looked into the distance. His feet had swelled up in his shoes during the long night, but they caused him no pain, only he could not move his toes much, they were too stiff.

As the night seemed to close in around him, he began to crawl toward the area where he had seen Netti sitting and contemplating. He felt his way carefully, not wanting to cause any noise. He began to think that the world was full of the crass-headed idiots and the poverty-stricken in spirit! He realized that people like Netti were probably devout Christians who bent their knees piteously before the church altar on Sundays. He thought to himself that every cell in his body mocked false piousness as practiced by the great deceivers. Thinking of Myrna swinging from the tree limb, he felt like shouting to a God in which he did not believe that he would scoff him on the day of doom, and curse the teeth out of his mouth for the sake of a selfish deity's ignoring the plight of such a good woman.

Suddenly, he realized he had crawled within a few feet of where Netti sat trying to stem the flow of blood from the piercing wound to his left arm. Aaron decided to wait. He was in no hurry. The hunter had now become the hunted without realizing it.

Netti was breathing heavily as the flow of blood from the wound trickled down his arm. He was scanning the horizon, but was obviously worried because there was no sign of Aaron and the quiet was almost deafening. He was in pain, and he was determined to make Aaron pay for that pain.

Winter in the New Jersey wetlands was cold, damp and harsh. It was now snowing very lightly. A foggy, dark, and everlasting night seemed to descend upon the two men facing off in a titanic battle of wills. Every slight noise in the still night seemed to be a clang of doom as each sound choked the night air.

Both men had observed every little detail of their surroundings, nothing was lost on them; their attention was acutely keen. Aaron grew more and more obsessed by this evil before him. What brought all this on he asked himself? Could he blame Jasmine for falling in love with Brent, which obviously created a situation where a man of such low character became obsessed once a woman of her stature actually considered him a worthy lover? No, she was simply overwhelmed with his good old boy charm. She was vulnerable at the time, and could not be blamed for succumbing to such a master manipulator. Now, with his arrest, she realized that she had been duped into loving a man with no core to his soul. She had learned the hard way that in many men beneath the surface lays the potential for evil.

Time seemed to crawl by as the men sat contemplating their next move. Netti had laid down the rifle, but he had his right hand on the Samurai sword, seemingly anticipating the wrath which he would bring forth from the razor sharp blade.

As Aaron, undetected, gazed up at a man of great physical strength, he palpably, vividly embodied before his eyes a man deformed of spirit who was repulsively tall, sinewy, and rather dark; with limbs like tree trucks. He was a formidable foe both physically and mentally.

Aaron now had the element of surprise on his side, as the wound Netti suffered, no doubt, had caused a temporary lapse in his assuredness. Aaron was leery of the sword, because a man who carried a samurai sword was obviously skilled in its use, because it was not a frivolous toy. In fact, Aaron feared the sword more than the rifle. It was meant to inflict pain, and that was what Netti enjoyed.

Time went. Aaron sank down lower to the ground, reached up and dried the sweat from his brow and throat, drew a couple of long breaths, and forced himself into calmness as he waited for the inevitable. Damn, he thought to himself, it's freezing out here and I am sweating. The moon slid behind a cloud and the darkness became almost complete. Aaron, exhausted from the ordeal, sank, simply sank in spirit and slipped into ignominy, feeling that he might never rise again from the ground upon which he lay. Was this to be the inglorious end to Aaron Adams?

He dragged himself up wet and exhausted, and gazed towards Netti who was breathing heavily, no doubt, enduring great pain from the wound. Did Netti know? Did he realize what Aaron had so brazenly done to the knife that pierced him? No, he did not know thought Aaron. He was unaware that, as he sat there waiting for Aaron, he had already lost the battle.

The Girl Who Motivated Murder Most Foul

Aaron struggled for breath, remembering two women.

Outside my heart I hear the gentle breeze,
As it caresses the few leaves from the tall trees,
And carries them on winter wind flittering around,
Then, they gently fall to the ground.

I see the darkness so high above,
Where owls make a deadly shove.
And laid upon their deadly wings
My death to you the night brings.

And as they start their deadly descent,
Delivering a message that's serenely sent,
I want you to know to me you are so dear
And I forlornly wish you were near.

Upon your soft breasts I would lay my head,
Letting my affection upon you spread.
I want to protect you from howling winds
But upon the frozen ground my life descends.

Visions of you dance in my mind
As you my dear were so kind.
I want to suck up your nectar so sweet,
And my loneliness and despair defeat.

You were my golden flower
You gave me power.
You brought my life purpose,

The Girl Who Motivated Murder Most Foul

But tomorrow they will find my carcass.

As the wind blows gently across the land
It is as if I hear the faint whisper in the sand.
It is a melody of merriment that fills my heart,
But then the veil of darkness gets a start.

I cannot have you by my side.
I cannot reach over and touch you where you lie,
Feel your softness, look upon your succulent,
wet lips that cry out for a tender kiss lovingly sent.

I cannot see you teasingly play the games
That makes my heart roar with soaring flames.
How I long to caress you so fondly and often.
The pain of this cold I wish you could soften.

Woe is me who must lie here in the cold.
You were my inspiration that that made me bold.
My heart knows you were the twinkle in my eyes;
You were the breath of life that now slowly dies.

Aaron could hear Netti's breathing getting heavier and more laboured. Aaron's breathing also was becoming laboured as the cold engulfed him and seemed to wrap him in its sombre embrace. His mind was racing now, wondering what people would say when they discovered his cold, lifeless body probably the next morning when passerby's noticed his car parked on the edge of the forest and notified authorities.

Of course, they would find two dead bodies, because Hiram Nettie would also be dead, dead from the deadly poison of the evergreen *Yew Bush* which Aaron had luckily found near the pit he dug. The tiny seeds harboured a deadly poison in which Aaron had dipped his pocket knife. Thanks to his grandmother, he had once been saved from certain death when he started to eat some of the toxic berries. Death could be almost instantaneous, but a man Netti's size would take a bit longer for the poison to take effect. However, as Aaron lay on the ground shivering from the cold, he watched Netti's head tilt to one side, and Aaron knew that Netti had paid for Myrna's death. It wasn't the hideous death Aaron had planned in retribution, but it was death nonetheless.

The cold embraced Aaron and he felt his body going numb. The moon popped from behind the cloud that had covered it and shone a light down into the forest. Aaron felt the glow on his body, closed his eyes and embraced eternity.

EPILOGUE
WHERE WAS HE?

I talk without speaking.
I listen without hearing.
I look without seeing.
I learn without knowing.
I touch without feeling.
Then I think of you
And suddenly the sun shines.
Birds sing and a soft breeze blows.
I get lost in memories
Of that which was golden.
Ah, I said we played out.
But the strings of that violin
Are threads to my heart.
Though we are now apart.

Jasmine sat forlornly that faithful night, wondering where Aaron was. He had told her about Myrna, but she understood his need to seek out solace from another woman. It was she who had driven him to another's arms. She knew that and understood it. When she had hinted at coming back to him, she could feel the love deep within him, but she could also sense the trepidation as he said, "Can you guarantee you won't do this again? My heart cannot take it. I am with a woman who seems to adore me, and I know it may only be transitory, but how I fear the pain of losing you again. It is more than I could bear."

Jasmine Alexander looked out at the darkness as snow was gently falling and thought to herself, "Why did this man find me so alluring that he was willing to commit murder to keep me?" She eased back into her chair, looked out at the darkness despondently and wondered what made her **The Girl Who Motivated Murder Most Foul!"**

**Don't miss these other Girl Series Books
By J. Wayne Frye:**

The Girl Who Said Goodbye for the Last Time
The Girl Who Stirred Up the Whirlwind
The Girl Who Danced with the Demons of Darkness
The Girl Who Made Love to the Yeti in Kathmandu

And these Aaron Adams mysteries:

Fall from Apocalypse
Armageddon Now
Something Evil in the Darkness at Hopkins House
When Jesus Came to Jersey as the Son of Thunder
When Jesus Came to Canada to Lead an Indigenous
Rebellion in the Broughton Archipelago

And The New Chablis Louis Chavez Thriller:

Chablis: Avenging Angel for the Forgotten
in the City of Lost Hope

**Available at your local bookstore or from
Amazon.com**